# Witch Is When Everything Went Crazy

Published by Implode Publishing Ltd
© Implode Publishing Ltd 2015

The right of Adele Abbott to be identified as the Author of the Work has been asserted by her in accordance with the Copyright, Designs and Patents Act 1988.

All rights reserved, worldwide.
No part of this publication may be reproduced, stored in a retrieval system, or transmitted, in any form or by any means without the prior written permission of the copyright owner.

The characters and events in this book are fictitious. Any similarity to real persons, dead or alive, is purely coincidental and not intended by the author.

# Chapter 1

"I love you so much." I sighed. "You're the only one for me. I'll never cheat on you, I promise."

"Jill, why are you talking to that custard cream?"

Oh, bum. I hadn't realised Kathy was back from the shops. I'd let myself into her place because I had a bone to pick with her.

"I wasn't talking to the biscuit. That would be crazy. I was just—err—I was humming."

"I think this biscuit obsession of yours is getting a bit out of hand. Maybe you should go and see someone about it."

"There's nothing wrong with me, and anyway, don't try to change the subject."

"What subject? I've only just walked in."

I gave her my dreaded death stare. I'd been practising in the mirror.

"Do you have tooth ache?"

No, I don't have toothache. This is my angry face."

"Why are you mad at me?"

"Like you don't know."

"Jill, you're freaking me out. What's wrong?"

"You rigged it," I said.

"Rigged what? What did I rig, and why do you look like you want to kill me?"

"The raffle. You rigged it so I'd win the date with Jack Maxwell."

She smiled. Guilty as charged.

My name is Jill Gooder, and I'm a private investigator. I'd taken over the family business after my adoptive father died. My life had become much more complicated when I'd discovered that I was a witch. I wasn't allowed to tell any human about the whole witch thing, and that included my adoptive sister, Kathy. The reason I was at her place that morning was to have it out with her for rigging a charity raffle, which had resulted in me going on a date with Detective Jack Maxwell, a man I'd hated almost as much as he'd hated me. As it turned out, the date had gone much better than I'd expected, but that didn't mean I was going to let Kathy off the hook.

"How did the date go?" She led me into the living room. Or as I'd come to know it: the room that the vacuum forgot.

"Never mind how it went." I turned to face her. "Why did you do it?"

"I didn't. Who says I did?" Her smile had turned into a grin.

"Jack Maxwell says you did."

"And you're going to take the word of Detective Jack Maxwell, the man who you supposedly hate, over the word of your loving sister?"

"Every day of the week."

She feigned hurt, but the grin didn't go away. "I may have *massaged* the results—but only a teensy weensy bit. Hardly at all really."

"So in other words, you rigged it?"

"Someone had to do something about you two. It's obvious to everyone that you have the hots for one another. I just helped love along a little. Even your names are compatible—"

"Don't you dare!"

"What?"

"If you recite that stupid nursery rhyme, I *will* kill you."

"Okay, okay. I won't recite any nursery rhyme that includes the names Jack and Jill. No hills will be mentioned. Or buckets. Empty or otherwise."

"Are you going to make me a coffee or what?"

"Only if you tell me how it went."

"Coffee first."

Kathy walked through to the kitchen, humming as she went.

"I can hear you."

"What?" She gave me that innocent look of hers.

"You're humming Jack and Jill. It isn't funny."

"Tell me how the date went, and I'll stop humming."

I was still trying to figure out how the so-called date had gone. I'd been determined to hate every second of it. I'd even offered to cancel, but Maxwell had said we should see it through. The night hadn't been the ordeal I'd been expecting. In fact, much to my surprise, I'd enjoyed his company. I'd seen another side to Detective Maxwell—a human side. By the end of the evening, I'd even begun to think that maybe— No! That was ridiculous.

"It wasn't as bad as I expected."

"What does that mean?"

"We didn't kill one another."

"That's a start I guess."

Kathy put the biscuit tin on the table between us. I gave her a look.

"What?"

I walked over to the cupboard, and took out a fresh packet of custard creams—my favourite.

"What's wrong with these?" She pointed to the biscuit tin.

I ignored her, and helped myself to two custard creams from the new packet. Kathy tried to make out there was something strange or unusual about my dislike for having biscuits mixed together. Digestives and custard creams—sharing the same tin? Yuk!

"Is there somewhere I can put these?" I held up the newly opened packet of custard creams.

"Sure, give them here." She snatched the packet, and tipped them into the biscuit tin. Evil—pure evil—that was my sister.

"I did find out one thing about Maxwell last night," I said, once I'd got over the biscuit travesty.

"He's a good kisser?"

"We did *not* kiss!"

"Not even a peck?"

I'd thought he was about to give me a goodnight peck on the cheek when Drake had shown up. Kathy didn't know anything about Drake, and I wasn't about to tell her. Not that there was much to tell, other than he was a wizard with a killer smile. I'd been out with him once, to a karaoke night in Candlefield, which was home to all manner of supernaturals. But I'm not sure you'd call it a date. Drake had mentioned that he planned to visit Washbridge, but when he showed up out of the blue like that when I was with Maxwell—let's just say it was a little awkward.

"I think I know why Maxwell dislikes P.I.s so much," I said. "Do you remember the Camberley kidnap case some time ago?"

"The heiress? She was found dead wasn't she?"

I nodded. "Maxwell was lead detective on that case. It seems that a P.I. working for the family spooked the kidnappers, and they killed their hostage."

"Why would he hold that against *you*?"

"I'm a P.I.—that's reason enough. At least now I know I'll try to tread a little more carefully around him."

"You? Tread carefully? Good luck with that one. Are you going to see him again?"

"I'm sure our paths will cross."

"I meant on another date."

"Unlikely."

I had thought that Maxwell was about to ask me out again, but then Drake had shown up, so I'd never know for sure.

"So, about your birthday," I said, pleased to change the subject.

"Everything's arranged." Kathy dunked a digestive biscuit into her coffee. Gross! "Pete has booked a day off work."

That wasn't what I'd been hoping to hear. Kathy and I had a tradition of spending our birthdays together—lots of alcohol was usually involved. This year though, I had a problem. I was double-booked. I'd only recently been reunited with my birth mother. That's when I'd found out that I was a witch—she'd told me on her death bed. Since then, my mother's ghost had been a regular visitor. She'd found herself a new man—well not exactly new—they'd been childhood sweethearts. Anyhow, his name was Alberto, and he was Welsh—don't ask. My mother and

Alberto were about to get married. And no, I hadn't realised that ghosts could get married either. Their wedding day was the same day as Kathy's birthday. I'd been hoping that I'd be able to persuade Kathy that we could celebrate her birthday on the day before or the day after, but I was too late, she'd already made arrangements for her husband, Peter, to take the day off work to look after the kids.

It was going to be a logistical nightmare. Even though time stood still in Washbridge, whenever I was in Candlefield, juggling the two events on the same day wasn't going to be easy. How did I get myself into these situations?

"That's great." I tried to sound enthusiastic.

"I'm going to get very, very drunk." Kathy grinned.

I didn't doubt it, if the last few birthdays were anything to go by.

As we walked across the living room, I stepped on something. Luckily for me, it wasn't one of the thousands of Lego pieces which were usually scattered across the carpet.

"What's this?" I held the offending item at arm's length.

"It's a bion."

"What's a bion?"

"Half bear, half lion — a bion."

Lizzie and Kathy had recently claimed my beanie collection. The collection that I'd treasured (to say nothing of catalogued) throughout my childhood and beyond.

"Who did *this*?"

"I did," Kathy said proudly. "Lizzie said she wanted a bion, so I—"

"Ripped two perfectly good beanies apart, and made this monster?"

"Cute, isn't he?"

'Cute' wasn't the first word that came to mind. The bion was a thing of nightmares. "These are my beanies."

"*Were*. They *were* your beanies—past tense. You gave them to your niece. Remember, Auntie Jill?"

I remembered them being taken by force. I remembered there being no concern for my feelings when I was left beanie-less. Apart from the squid of course. He was secreted away. Safe from the hands of these beanie torturers.

"This is just plain cruel," I said.

"You don't think that maybe you're over-reacting a little?"

I threw the beanie-monster behind the sofa, so I wouldn't have to look at it.

"How are Peter, Mikey and the little torturer of beanies?"

Kathy ignored my jibe. "Everyone's fine. Looking forward to our mini-break."

The local social club had organised a long weekend to Lewton-on-Sea. There were so many people going on the trip that they'd been able to get a substantial discount on the hotel and funfair for the block booking. It sounded like my idea of hell, but Kathy, Peter and the kids were beside themselves with excitement.

I bought a copy of the Bugle in the forlorn hope that Dougal Andrews, a creep of a journalist, had printed an apology for the article he'd published about me and the local police. Today's headline was 'Jewel and the

Clown'—the Bugle loved its puns—about a bungled jewel heist. Needless to say, there was no sign of an apology.

Colonel Briggs was waiting for me in the outer office. He looked every inch the retired military man except perhaps for the purple and orange scarf around his neck. My PA/receptionist, Mrs V, spent most of her day knitting. She specialised in scarves, and was something of a celebrity in local knitting circles. She'd even won a competition, and to prove it, the trophy sat proudly on top of the stationery cupboard, opposite her desk.

"Colonel Briggs?" I offered my hand.

"Pleased to meet you, Ma'am."

"Please call me Jill. Shall we go through to my office?"

"Lead the way." He turned to Mrs V. "Thank you for the fine neck-wear, young lady."

Young lady? Was he flirting with Mrs V? She could do worse.

"I say," Colonel Briggs said. "He's a handsome thing."

I glanced around the room. He couldn't mean—

"Reminds me of Tinker. My old Corporal."

I'd heard Winky called many things, but handsome was not one of them. Winky was the one-eyed cat I'd adopted from the cat re-homing centre. At least, that was my version of events. According to him, *he'd* adopted *me*. Since inheriting my witch powers, I'd been able to talk to Winky which hadn't always been a positive experience. Of late, he'd taken to wearing an eye patch, but didn't have it on this morning.

"Tinker lost his eye going over the top," the colonel said. "Shrapnel. What about him? How did he lose his?" He pointed to Winky.

"Not shrapnel as far as I know." It occurred to me I'd never actually asked what happened to his eye.

"Who's this crazy old coot?" Winky said. Fortunately, the colonel heard only a series of meows.

I ignored Winky, and led the colonel over to my desk. "How can I help, Colonel? Mrs V mentioned something about a charity for dogs?"

Winky hissed. I gave him a look.

"That's right. I'm president of Washbridge Dog Rescue."

Winky hissed again.

The colonel continued, "We rely on donations to fund our work. The majority of our income comes from bequests. Recently, one of our most enthusiastic supporters, Mrs Edna Vicars, passed away. She'd told me on several occasions that she planned to change her Will, so that the charity would be the major beneficiary. In fact, we spoke only a few days before her untimely death."

"Untimely?"

"Edna was in her eighties, but still going strong except for a touch of angina. If I get my hands on whoever did it."

"What happened?"

"She was hit by a car right outside her house. The coward didn't even have the courage to stop and face up to what he'd done."

"Hit and run? That's terrible. I'm sorry."

"She died before she could change her Will, and I'm absolutely sure that it was one of her damn kids who ran her down."

"That's a very serious accusation. Do you have any proof?"

"Not a thing, but I'm a good judge of character, and that son of hers—Hector—total waste of space. And from what I hear, her daughter isn't much better."

"What do the police say?"

"They're trying to trace the driver. Not trying hard enough for my liking. That's why I want you on the job. I saw the article in the Bugle, so I know you share my disillusionment with the local plod."

"That article, I didn't actually—"

"This is extremely important to me. Edna was a very dear friend. It isn't just about the money. I want to see her killer brought to justice."

"What about my fees? Can the charity afford—?"

"The charity won't be paying, I will. What do you say, young lady? Will you help a frail old man?"

Colonel Briggs was many things, but frail wasn't one of them. He still looked as though he could handle himself if the going got tough.

"It would be an honour."

# Chapter 2

I could hear Grandma's voice when I was only halfway up the stairs to my office. I seriously considered turning around and making a run for it, but if I knew Grandma, she'd already know I was there, and I'd be in big trouble. Grandma was the head of my birth family with whom I'd only recently been reunited. I was now in regular contact with an aunt: Aunt Lucy, two cousins: Amber and Pearl, and the aforementioned Grandma. She was the only witch I'd met so far who actually looked how I'd always imagined a witch would look—warty nose and all. On a scale of one to scary, she was an eleven. And to make matters worse, she'd decided that she should be the one to oversee my education in all things witchy.

Grandma had been to my office before. On that occasion, she and Mrs V had been on a night out together, and they'd both got very drunk. Boomerangs and boxer shorts had been involved.

"Grandma!" I forced my best smile. "What a pleasant surprise."

She gave me her 'look', turned to Mrs V, and said, "See how my own granddaughter lies to me." She looked back at me. "You're late."

"Late?"

"It's five past nine."

"This is *my* business," I managed, weakly.

"That's no excuse. The sign on the door says nine am to six pm. So, you're late."

"Sorry." Why was I apologising? That was the kind of effect she had on me. "What are you doing here?"

"Aren't I allowed to visit my granddaughter?"

"Of course. I just wasn't expecting to see you."

"I was just telling Annabel—"

"Who?"

Mrs V coughed. I kept forgetting Annabel was her first name. She'd always be Mrs V to me.

"Mrs V, of course."

"As I was saying." Grandma fixed me with her gaze. "I've been telling Annabel about my new venture."

"That's nice."

"Aren't you going to ask me what it is?"

"Sorry. What's your new venture?"

"I'm glad you asked. I've done my research, and discovered there's a shortage of yarn outlets in this area."

"That's true." Mrs V nodded.

"A gap in the market, you might say." Grandma grinned—not a pretty sight. "I plan to fill that gap."

It took a few seconds for her words to sink in. Surely she couldn't mean what I thought she meant.

"So? What do you think?" she asked.

"Well. That sounds—I mean it's obviously—"

"Come on, girl. Spit it out. What do you think?"

"Does that mean—?" Please no—anything but this. "Does that mean you're planning to open a shop in Washbridge?"

"Exactly."

"A wool shop?"

"I can see why you're a private investigator. Nothing gets past you, does it?"

"Do you have the time to run a shop? I mean—err—I know how busy you are already."

"Haven't you heard the saying: 'If you want something

doing ask a busy man'?"

"Didn't Benjamin Franklin say that?"

"No, I did, just now. Didn't you hear me?" She turned towards the outer door. "Now come on."

"Me?"

"Who else?"

"Where are we going?"

"I've set up a number of viewings. You can come along and give me a second opinion."

"Viewings? Of shops?"

"No, of camels. Of course, of shops. Now, are you coming or what?"

The young man who showed us around the various properties had a lot to say—too much if Grandma's expression was anything to go by.

"This property has only recently come onto the market. It is ideally situated—"

I'd been daydreaming, but was suddenly snapped back to earth.

"That's better," Grandma said.

"What have you done to him?"

The man was frozen like a statue—his mouth open mid-sentence.

"He was giving me a headache," Grandma said.

"Will he be alright?"

"Of course. It's not permanent. The 'freeze' spell will only last for a few minutes. We'll be gone before he comes around."

I'd completed my level one witch training, and was about to embark on the next level. I was looking forward to it, but not to the lessons with Grandma. There were six levels in all. My cousins, Amber and Pearl, were on level two, and they'd been in training since they were born, so I guessed I was doing okay. I had a long way to go to catch up with Grandma though. As a level six witch, she was as powerful as they come.

"Are you coming or not?" Grandma was waiting by the door.

I glanced back at the frozen man, and then followed her outside.

"So? Which one do you think?" she asked.

"I think this one is the best we've seen."

"So do I. It's just the right size. Now, all I have to do is come up with a name. How about 'Yarnstorming'? Or 'Ever a Wool Moment'? What do you think?"

"What about 'Stitch Slapped'?"

"I don't think so."

"Are you absolutely sure you want to do this?" I said. "You aren't getting any—" Whoa! What was I saying? Did I have some kind of death wish?

"You were saying?" Grandma's gaze burned into me.

"I was just—I mean—nothing. This one is the right size, and it's in a good location on a busy street. There's only one thing—"

"The bus stop?"

"Yeah." The bus stop was located right outside the shop. While we'd been looking around, the queue of people at the stop had blocked the window. "It's a pity because everything else is fine."

"I can sort that out." Grandma turned back to face the bus stop, and before I could ask what she was going to do, she did it.

The bus stop slid along the pavement until it was in

front of the bookmaker's, two doors down from the future wool emporium.

"That's better," she declared, happy with her work.

I glanced around to see if anyone had noticed, but everyone seemed to be going about their business as if it was the most natural thing in the world to see a bus stop relocate itself. I must have looked puzzled because Grandma said, "I cast the 'move' spell together with the 'mask' spell. Both are level four. The second spell is used to hide another spell. That's why no one noticed the bus stop moving."

The more I learned about magic, the more intrigued I became. I couldn't help but wonder what level I might have been on if I'd started on my studies when I was a kid.

The 'mask' spell had obviously worn off because I noticed an old lady do a double-take when she realised that the bus stop was now fifteen yards further down the road.

Peter had taken the kids to a birthday party — there seemed to be one almost every week. Kathy had invited me over for a takeaway. She had curry; I had burger and chips. I told her that Grandma was about to open a shop on the high street.

"How old is she?" Kathy said, through a mouthful of rice.

"I don't actually know. She can't possibly be as old as she looks."

"Shouldn't she have retired by now, and anyway how is she going to get here every day? Does she drive?"

Only a broomstick. "I'm not sure. By bus, I guess."

"Do you think she might find me a part-time job? For while the kids are at school."

This was going from bad to worse. The thought of those two working together didn't bear thinking about. "I doubt she'll be able to afford anyone at first."

"Ask her to keep me in mind, would you?"

"Sure." Not a chance.

"Have you heard from Jacky Boy?" Kathy asked.

"If you mean Maxwell, then no. Thank goodness."

"If you and he don't get together soon, I'll be forced to set you up on another blind date."

Kathy's track record at hooking me up on blind dates was less than stellar. If I told you that the guy who had spent all evening with his finger up his nose had been the 'pick' of the bunch, you'd probably get the picture.

"If you do, I'll kill you."

"I'm looking forward to my birthday blast. It's ages since I got off my face."

"Me too. I can't wait," I lied. Normally, I would have been looking forward to it, but I had the small matter of having to juggle that, and the wedding on the same day.

"Auntie Jill!" Mikey came rushing in.

"Auntie Jill." Lizzie was two steps behind him.

"Hi guys. How was the birthday party?"

"It was fantastic," Mikey said.

Lizzie nodded in agreement.

"There was a magician. He did magic tricks. It was fantastic. Can I have a magic set, Mum? Please?"

"You'll have to wait until Christmas. Money doesn't grow on trees you know."

"If I had a magic set, I could make it grow on trees." Mikey laughed. "Do you like magic, Auntie Jill?"

"I do." More than you'll ever know.

"You used to hate magic when we were kids," Kathy said. "You used to say it was fake."

Mikey looked horrified.

"I never said that," I protested.

"You did. Can't you remember that time when we were watching a magician at the seaside somewhere, and you stood up and shouted, 'It's in your hand'?"

"I never did that." The memories came flooding back. El Mystero, the so-called magician, had palmed a ball in one hand while pretending to make it vanish into thin air in the other. Such an amateur! "Anyway, I like magic now."

Mikey's smile returned. "Do you think magic is real, Auntie Jill?"

"Magic? Yes, I'm sure it is."

Peter hadn't spoken a word, which wasn't like him at all. Kathy must have noticed too because she sent the kids to play in their rooms.

"What's up?" Kathy said.

"The holiday money has gone."

"Gone? What do you mean, gone?"

"Norman Reeves has vanished, and taken the money with him."

"Where's he gone?" Kathy said.

"If I knew that, he wouldn't have vanished, would he?"

"No need to get ratty with me."

"Sorry. I just don't know how I'm going to tell the kids. They'll be devastated."

"Who's Norman Reeves?" I asked.

"He's the trip coordinator. Quiet guy. Works at the local housing office. I can't say I know him all that well. If I'm honest, he comes across as a little weird."

"Why would you trust him to be treasurer then?"

"He'd done it for the last two years. There's never been a problem before."

"If it helps, I could lend you the money," I said.

"Thanks, but it wouldn't do any good," Peter slumped down in the armchair. "Everyone's money has gone, so the whole thing will have to be called off."

Kathy put her head in her hands. "What are we going to tell them?" She gestured towards the kids' bedrooms.

Peter shook his head. "Let's give it a couple of days to see if anything turns up."

"I can't believe Norman would do something like that," Kathy said. "When was the last time anyone heard from him?"

"Two days ago, I think. He went to Antonio's for a meal with his girlfriend. Since then, nothing."

"Do you want me to see if I can come up with anything?" I offered.

"Do you think you can find him?" Peter looked hopeful.

"I don't know, but I'll give it my best shot."

"You have to find him, Jill." Kathy took my hand. "The kids will be devastated if the holiday is cancelled."

No pressure then.

I was becoming more sensitive to the presence of ghosts, and could usually tell now when my mother was close by.

"Mum?" I glanced around the living room of my flat. "Mum?"

"It's me," a male voice said.

I turned around to see Alberto. "What are you doing here? Is Mum alright?" Weird question, I know. She's dead—how much less alright could she be?

"Your mother is fine. Well, maybe a little upset."

"Why what's wrong?"

"You have to promise not to let her know I told you."

"Told me what?"

He hesitated.

"I promise I won't tell her. What's wrong?"

"On her death bed, your great-grandmother gave your mother her wedding ring. Your mother wore it on a necklace all of the time. She'd always planned to take it as her own wedding ring if she ever married again, but now she can't."

"Why not? What happened to it?"

"It's disappeared. She was wearing it when she went into the nursing home, but since she—" He couldn't bring himself to say the words.

"Died and came back as a ghost?"

He nodded. "It wasn't on her finger. I told her she should ask you to investigate, but she doesn't want to add to your workload."

"Leave it with me. I'm on it."

"Thank you, Jill. I knew you'd want to help. I won't say anything to your mother just in case you draw a blank. I don't want to get her hopes up."

# Chapter 3

At this rate, I was going to have to take on an assistant. As well as the Colonel Briggs case, I now had two other items on my to-do list: the missing holiday cash and the missing ring. The trouble was that two out of those three were unpaid, so maybe the assistant would have to wait.

"Why are you ordering treats for that horrible cat?" Mrs V asked when I walked into the office the next morning.

"What treats? I haven't ordered anything."

Mrs V passed me a parcel. It was addressed to 'Winky the Cat' care of my office address.

"Someone must have ordered them." Mrs V huffed. "It's bad enough you waste your money on premium cat food and full cream milk."

"It has to be a mistake. I'll look into it."

I'd no sooner stepped into my office, than Winky was all over me. "Did I hear 'treats'?"

I was too busy to worry about why someone would have sent Winky a parcel of cat treats. They were here now, so he might as well enjoy them. I ripped open the packet, and scattered a few on the floor. "Don't eat them all—" Too late. He'd already vacuumed them up.

"More!" he insisted.

What the heck? Anything to keep him quiet. I threw them to all four corners of the room. If he was going to eat them, he'd at least have to work for them.

"You couldn't just put them in my bowl?" he complained.

The last time I'd called this number seemed like a lifetime ago. Back then, I'd known nothing about my 'other' family, and I'd been oblivious to the fact that I was a witch.

"Daleside Nursing Home."

"Hi. My name is Jill Gooder. My mother passed away in your nursing home a few months ago. I want to speak to someone about a ring she was wearing."

"Hold the line please. I'll put you through to Admin."

The woman in Admin took my mother's details and my phone number, and promised to give me a call back after she'd checked their records. She assured me that any jewellery on the deceased was always recorded and accounted for.

The rest of the day was taken up chasing down the children of Mrs Vicars. Neither of them seemed too keen to talk to me until I turned on the charm offensive. What? I can do charm when I need to. In the end, I'd managed to set up appointments to see them both.

I also managed to catch up with my accounts—a job I enjoyed about as much as a visit to the dentist.

Peter called to tell me that the newly formed Action Committee had arranged a meeting. In my experience an Action Committee usually meant a 'talk a lot, but do nothing remotely useful' committee. I said I'd attend anyway.

A couple of days earlier, the twins had sent me a message to say that they'd finally found the courage to tell Aunt Lucy about their engagements. Despite their apprehension, she'd been delighted, and had insisted on organising a family dinner to celebrate. I was invited. The meal was at Aunt Lucy's, but the message hadn't made it clear if Grandma would be there. Maybe she'd be too busy with her new wool shop venture. I could always hope.

I arrived in Candlefield a few hours before the dinner was due to start. I'd spent all day on the phone chasing my own tail, and needed to wind down.

The twins were working in Cuppy C. Barry was lying in the corridor upstairs, and came bounding over the moment he caught sight of me.

"Let's go for a walk. Can we? Can we?"

I couldn't refuse the big, soft thing, but I fancied a change from the park. I still found it surprising how warm and welcoming most of the inhabitants seemed to be. Everyone I encountered along the way said hello, and many of them knew my name. Maybe humans could learn a thing or two from sups?

After an hour or so, I found myself in the market square. It was much quieter than on my previous visit. I daren't venture into the heart of the market because Barry was showing way too much interest in the food on offer. Instead, I skirted around the edge. About halfway around, one stall caught my eye: 'Spell Accessories - everything for the busy witch/wizard'. That was me—I was run off my feet. There was no food stall nearby, so I felt safe taking a closer look.

There was all manner of gizmos, many of which I didn't understand. One thing that caught my eye was something called a 'Stor-a-Spell'. These were small trinkets which came in a variety of shapes. As far as I could make out, they allowed you to cast a spell which the trinket would then store for a set period of time before activating it. I could definitely see how that might be useful.

Further along the row was a stall selling pet food and toys. Barry was more than a little interested in the food, but I managed to hold him at bay while I purchased a squeaky plastic bone.

"What's that?" Barry said.

"It's a toy for you."

"Can I eat it?"

"No, you mustn't eat it. It'll make you poorly. It's for you to play with. Here." I dropped the toy at his feet.

It had no sooner hit the ground than he grabbed it between his teeth, which made it squeak. Just as quickly, he dropped it and scrambled behind my legs.

"Don't like it!" he whimpered.

"It's only a toy."

"Don't like it."

"There's a little squeaker inside. It can't hurt you."

"Don't like it."

Oh well. That was money well spent.

Grandma was seated at the head of the table—she'd made it to the engagement party despite the demands of her new business enterprise—oh goody. William and Alan, who were seated next to their fiancées, looked as nervous as kittens. Lester, Aunt Lucy's new love interest, looked relieved not to be the one under the spotlight for a change.

"Why did you bring these young men here today?" Grandma asked.

Amber and Pearl exchanged a nervous glance. "To celebrate our engagement, Grandma."

"I know that. I'm not stupid. I meant why would you want to expose them to your mother's cooking? Aren't you worried it will scare them off?"

Aunt Lucy gave Grandma a look of disdain, but said nothing.

"Mum is a very good cook," Amber said.

Pearl looked aghast at her sister—no doubt wondering when she'd developed a death wish.

"So, William and Alan." Grandma's gaze switched between the newcomers. "Why?"

William's Adam's apple did a jig, as he looked to Amber for help. She shrugged. He took a sip of water. "Why what?" he said, nervously.

"Why did you wait until now to tell us that you were engaged?"

William looked again at Amber who this time attempted to come to his rescue.

"We announced it as soon as we could."

I looked at Pearl and Alan. They were both staring down at the table.

"Really?" Grandma said, looking at both the twins now. "That's not what I heard. I heard that you have both been engaged for some time."

Busted!

"Yes, well," Amber stuttered. "We did actually get engaged a little while ago—"

"We had meant to—" Pearl said.

"How come I didn't know?" Aunt Lucy said.

"Because you were too busy smooching with Moustache Man over there to notice." Grandma threw a glance Lester's way. He began to twizzle his moustache nervously.

"You haven't been wearing a ring—either of you." Aunt Lucy challenged her daughters.

How I loved these convivial dinners.

"Oh but they did," Grandma said. "Just not when you were around."

That woman saw all—knew all.

"Sorry, Mum." Amber bowed her head.

"Sorry, Mum," Pearl said.

Grandma cleared her throat.

"Sorry, Grandma," they chorused.

"Oh well," Aunt Lucy said. "It's official now, so let's toast the happy couples."

We all raised our glasses—even Grandma.

"To Amber and William, and Pearl and Alan." Aunt Lucy proposed the toast.

"Amber and William, and Pearl and Alan." Everyone clinked their glasses together except Grandma who was already halfway down hers.

Despite Grandma's warnings about the food, the meal was delicious, and thoroughly enjoyed by everyone—including Grandma, even though she'd never have admitted it.

"Who will you go to your mum's wedding with?" Pearl asked when we were on dessert.

"I'll be on my lonesome," I said, scooping up a spoonful of jam roll and custard. "Unless, I can bring Barry."

"Sorry, no animals allowed." Aunt Lucy laughed. "What about the man you went to the karaoke with. What was his name again?"

"Drake. Drake Tyson."

"How do I know that name?" Grandma said.

I shrugged. "I don't really know him all that well. We met when I was walking Barry."

"You should get in touch with him," Pearl said. "Ask him to go with you."

"We'll see."

I was relieved to hear a knock on the door. Anything to divert attention away from me.

Pearl went to see who was there.

"Oh hello?" I heard her say. "Did you want to see Jill? Why don't you come through?"

"Well, well," Grandma said. "Look who it is."

I *was* looking, and the puzzled expression on my face must have matched that on Drake's.

"Hello everyone," he said.

"We were just talking about you." Grandma's smile was more scary than reassuring. "Were your ears burning?"

Drake stuttered something unintelligible.

"Grab a chair." Aunt Lucy came to his rescue. "You've missed dinner, I'm afraid, but there's plenty of jam roll and custard."

"Thanks." He took the seat beside me. "I love jam roll and custard."

"Hi," I said.

"Hi yourself."

"I wasn't expecting to see *you* here today."

"I wasn't expecting to *be* here. One minute I was wondering what to put in the microwave, and the next I was knocking on your door."

I turned to look at Grandma. She smiled a knowing smile.

Despite the manner in which he'd been delivered to the house, I was glad of Drake's company.

After getting his bearings, he seemed happy to join in the celebrations.

"Will you be taking Jill to the wedding?" Grandma asked.

I gave her a death stare—like she'd even notice—or care.

"Wedding?" Drake looked at me.

"My mother's. My late mother's." Man this was complicated.

"She's a ghost?" He helped me out.

"Yeah. She's marrying Alberto. Her childhood sweetheart."

"Is he Italian?"

"Welsh."

"Of course."

"So, Drake." Grandma hadn't done with us yet. "Will you be taking Jill to the wedding or not?"

Floor, please open up and swallow me—right now.

"It would be my pleasure." Drake smiled. "If that's okay with you?" He looked to me for approval.

"Of course it's okay with her," Grandma said. "She's got no one else to go with."

And while you're at it, floor, open up and swallow Grandma as well.

"Don't forget I can read your mind, young lady."

I'd been excused washing up, and had managed to manoeuvre Drake out into the garden where I thought we might have some privacy.

"I'm sorry about that," I said. "You don't have to go to the wedding if you don't want to. Grandma can be a bit of a bully."

"I *do* want to." He took my hand. "Provided you haven't already planned to go with someone else."

"Didn't you hear what Grandma said? No one else wants to take me."

"I don't believe that for a moment, but if you'd like me to accompany you, it would be my pleasure."

"Okay. It's a date then. Well, not a *date* date, more of an *appointment*."

"Appointment? How romantic." He laughed.

"You know what I mean. It's good of you to take me, but it doesn't mean it has to be a date—I'll shut up, shall I?"

"Yeah. Quit while you're behind."

After Drake had left, Pearl and Amber caught up with me.

"Do you like him?" Pearl asked.

"Yeah, he's nice. You do realise that Grandma magicked him here, don't you?"

"We guessed. He didn't know which way was up when I answered the door."

"Still it'll be nice for us all to have partners for the wedding," Amber said.

I managed a smile, but was worried that this might make my juggling act with Kathy's birthday even more difficult.

# Chapter 4

Level two spells were—well—a whole new level. Although I was excited to have moved up, I was terrified that I'd mess up big time in front of Grandma.

Somehow, I had to find time to practise, but it wasn't easy with all the cases, paid and unpaid, which were starting to stack up. I'd set the alarm an hour earlier than usual, so I could devote a little time to magic before I set off to the office.

Grandma did at least give me prior warning of the spells which we'd be focussing on in each lesson. I was fortunate that I found memorising the mental images fairly easy now. Amber and Pearl had both admitted that they still struggled to commit spells to memory quickly, which probably explained why they'd been stuck on level two for so long.

It took only a matter of seconds to memorise the first ever level two spell which I tackled, but when I tried to cast the spell, nothing happened. The spell that was causing me so much grief was called 'listen'. It was meant to give me super enhanced hearing for a period of five minutes, but so far—nothing. I thought maybe I'd mixed up the images, but I double and triple checked, and still it didn't work.

"What's wrong with you?" I shouted at the book of spells. Maybe there was a mistake in the book. Maybe the wrong image had been listed or the sequence was wrong. Was there some kind of help desk I could call? I could just picture it:

*'Book of spells - your call is important to us - you are twenty-thousandth in the queue.'*

If I messed up, could Grandma drop me back down to level one? She could, and she would. Or she might do something much worse.

"Help!" I screamed in frustration.

"You called?"

I almost jumped out of my skin. My mother's ghost was hovering in front of me. She looked concerned. "Are you okay, Jill?"

"Yeah, sorry. I'm just struggling with this spell, and I'm worried what Grandma might do."

"Is this your first attempt at a level two spell?"

I nodded. "Maybe it's too soon for me to move up."

"Nonsense. Remember you've already performed spells well above level two."

"Yeah, but I messed those up."

"I'm not so sure you did."

"I can't understand why it won't work. Could the book be wrong?"

My mother gave me a look.

"I guess not." I sighed.

"Whatever you do, don't say that to Grandma. It wouldn't go down well."

"So why isn't it working? I'm sure I have the images memorised correctly."

"There's much more to being a witch than simply being able to memorise the spells. As Grandma so eloquently puts it: 'Any half-wit can remember a spell'. At level one, you can get away with simply being able to remember the spell, but as you move up the levels it becomes more about the execution—the focus on the desired outcome. Do you remember when you used the 'shrink' spell?"

How could I forget? I'd been trying on a dress in a shop's changing room when it had become well and truly stuck. I'd used the spell to shrink myself, so I could get out of it, but I hadn't anticipated that I'd end up totally naked when my underwear also fell from my tiny body.

"You saw that?" I blushed.

"Don't worry. It's a common mistake." She smiled. "Although it doesn't always have such embarrassing results."

I'd felt bad enough at the time. If I'd realised my mother was watching, I'd have been totally mortified.

"That's a perfect example of why focus on the desired outcome is so important. It's what separates the most powerful witches from the rest. What had your desired outcome been?"

"To get out of the dress without losing my underwear." I was still wincing at the memory.

"If you'd focussed on precisely that outcome, then your underwear would have shrunk along with you. With any given spell, there is often a certain amount of flexibility. It's up to you to use your focus to achieve the outcome you desire. Do you remember the focus you applied when you performed the level five spell? You must bring that same level of focus to every spell from now on. Do you see?"

"I think so."

"Give it another try then."

I closed my eyes and shut out everything else. I was no longer aware of my mother's presence or even of the room around me. Every ounce of my concentration was focussed on executing the spell. I didn't even have to think about the sequence of the images, it was as if my memory was on auto-pilot.

"Ouch! Ouch!" I clamped my hands over my ears to muffle the sounds that were assaulting them from every direction. I could hear a dozen different voices. The birds in the garden seemed to be singing through megaphones.

My mother's voice cut through the chatter. "Focus on one sound. Filter out everything else."

I closed my eyes again, and focussed only on her voice. Slowly every other sound faded into the background.

"That's it," she said in a whisper that almost burst my ear drums. "You should be okay now."

"Thanks," I said, but she'd already disappeared.

I'd have to learn how to control this particular spell, or I'd end up with perforated ear drums. In the time remaining before the spell wore off, I decided to try to pick up on a single conversation. From the background chatter, I picked out one conversation in particular.

"Ooh, Ivy. You're so sexy."

Hmm. Maybe I should tune this one out before it became embarrassing.

"My little Candy-floss."

What? It couldn't be. Was I suffering some kind of side-effect from the spell? I'd recognise that voice anywhere. Mr Ivers was one of my neighbours, and someone I did my best to avoid. He was a film buff who had a degree in boring.

"Ooh Ivy. Your eyebrows are so hot."

Ivy? Who called Mr Ivers, Ivy? Hot eye brows? He had a mono-brow. And, who on earth was Candy-floss?

Before I could learn any more, the spell had worn off, and my hearing had returned to normal.

I simply couldn't take in what I'd just heard. It was hard enough to imagine Mr Ivers with a woman—any woman—but to hear her getting hot and bothered about his mono-brow—I must have been high.

Even though I couldn't get rid of the image of Mr Ivers and his hot mono-brow, I was pleased to have mastered the spell.

As I left the flat, I heard voices. Walking towards me along the corridor was Mr Ivers. On his arm was a voluptuous young woman, with orange hair and matching lips. The two of them were laughing and chatting—totally oblivious to my presence. Normally, I'd have slipped back into my flat to avoid him, but I was too stunned to move. As they squeezed past me, I said, "Morning, Mr Ivers."

He glanced my way, but didn't speak. As they walked away I heard the woman say," Who was that Ivy?"

"No one, Candy-floss," he replied. "Just some woman who keeps bothering me."

I felt as though I'd slipped into another dimension. I'd been blanked by Mr Ivers. That was an all time low even for me. And who on earth was Candy-floss?

I was still reeling from my encounter with Ivy and Candy-floss when I arrived at the office. If an alien space ship had been parked outside, I couldn't have been any more stunned than I already was.

"Have you taken any of my scarves?" Mrs V greeted me.

"No, why?"

"Some are missing."

How could she tell? The cupboard was creaking under the weight of them, and every drawer in her desk was full of them too.

"You do give a lot of them away." To every visitor whether they wanted one or not.

"There are definitely three missing. Someone's been in my cupboard. You should investigate."

"Investigate?"

"It's what you do isn't it?"

"Yeah. Sure. I'll add it to my list." My ever growing list of unpaid cases. Maybe I should re-register as a charity?

I'd put off the call for as long as I could. Since my 'date' with Jack Maxwell, and after finding out about the Camberley case, I'd wanted to try to clear the air—professionally speaking. We hadn't had the best of working relationships—understatement of the year? I was nervous because I had no idea what kind of reception I might get. Would I get the version of Maxwell I'd seen on our 'date'? The one who'd been charming and easy to talk to. Or would I get the other Jack Maxwell? The one I'd come to know and hate; the one who looked at me like I was something he'd trodden in.

"Detective Maxwell, please."

"Who's calling?" said a bored voice on the other end of the phone.

"This is Jill Gooder."

Now for the moment of truth. Was I still on his black list? I tapped my fingers nervously on the desk.

"Hello?"

His voice took me by surprise. I'd expected to be told he was unavailable or at best, that he'd get back to me.

"Detective Maxwell?"

"How very formal. I thought we were on first name terms now."

"Sorry. *Jack*. I wasn't expecting you to—"

"What?"

"It doesn't matter. Look, I wondered if you could spare me a few minutes today?"

"How does ten-thirty sound? I can give you fifteen minutes then."

"Ten-thirty? Fine. I'll be there. Thanks."

That had gone better than I could have hoped. Maybe Kathy had done me a favour by rigging the raffle after all.

"If it isn't too much trouble." Winky said, as he jumped onto the chair opposite me. "Do you think I could get some food? I'm starving. And some milk too—before you dash off to see lover boy."

"Don't call him that."

"Jack and Jill went up the—" He jumped off the chair just in time to avoid the ruler I threw at him.

"No need for violence," he said.

"My relationship with Detective Maxwell is strictly professional."

"If you say so. 'Jack fell down and'—"

"I have a stapler and I'm not afraid to use it."

"You should have heard yourself on the phone just now." Winky mocked, "*I wonder if you could spare me a few minutes today*. You sounded like love's young dream."

Winky did a scarily accurate impression of me.

"That's rubbish."

"If you say so. Now, how about that food?"

Love's young dream? What nonsense. What did he know? And why was I having this debate with a cat?

Mrs V handed me a sheet of paper as I made my way out of the office.

"What's this?"

"It's a description of the missing scarves. I thought you'd need it when you put out an APB."

"APB? Right, thanks. I'm off to see Detective Maxwell."

"Such a nice man. Don't you think you should change first?"

"Change?"

"You look a little—dowdy—maybe something a little more alluring?"

"This is strictly business. I'll be fine."

"If you say so, dear. Maybe he can help to find the missing scarves."

"I'll be sure to run it by him."

It was such a beautiful day that I decided to walk to the police station. As I passed by the bus stop, I did a double take. The shop that Grandma and I had visited only a couple of days before had been totally transformed. The sign read 'Ever a Wool Moment'—I still preferred 'Stitch Slapped'. The interior of the shop had been decorated, carpeted and refitted with new shelving and a counter. On the floor were dozens of boxes—some of them open. Two young women were busy stocking the shelves with wool of every colour. I pressed my nose to the glass to get a better view. One of the women noticed me, smiled, and mouthed the words 'we open tomorrow'. I smiled back. There was no sign of Grandma, but somehow she'd managed to transform the shop, hire staff and was all set to open. How had she managed that? Magic must have been involved.

# Chapter 5

The last time we'd been in that interview room, Jack Maxwell and I had fought like cat and dog. I wondered how long the current uneasy peace between us would last.

"Jill," Jack said, as he entered the room.

"Jack. Thanks for seeing me."

"I'm afraid I don't have long." He took the seat opposite me.

"That's okay. I wondered if we might clear the air."

"What did you have in mind?"

"The other night. On our—"

"Date?" He smiled. "Did you set the gerbils on your sister?"

"Apparently, there's a world shortage of rabid gerbils—who knew? Anyway, the other night, you mentioned Camberley."

Suddenly more serious, he said, "What about it?"

"I know what happened with the family's private investigator."

"Look, I'd rather not get into that."

"I can understand why you have such a down on P.I.s after Camberley, but we aren't all the same."

"Are you sure about that? It seems to me you do pretty much what you want, and to hell with the law."

So much for the peace accord.

"I admit I can be a little headstrong at times."

"A little?"

"Okay, a lot. But I'd never do anything that would jeopardise someone's life in the way that happened in the Camberley case."

"Does that mean you'll stay out of police business?"

"I can't promise that."

"What then?"

It was a good question—what exactly did I have to offer?

"I want to work *with* you not *against* you," I said. "If I have any information that I think will help your investigations, I promise to pass it on."

"You should do that anyway."

"Look, I'm trying to make the peace. If you'd rather we carry on as before then—"

"No. I don't want that. I'm prepared to give it a try, but if you get in my way or if I think you are putting anyone in danger, then all deals are off."

"That's fair. Which brings me to the reason for my visit."

"Why do I get the feeling I'm not going to like this?"

"I'm doing what I said I'd do. I'm trying to work with you."

"I'm listening."

"Do you know about the hit and run? Mrs Vicars?"

He nodded. "We're trying to trace the driver, but we don't have much to go on. The only information we do have came from the next door neighbour, but she didn't actually see the incident."

"I've been hired by Colonel Briggs to look into it."

"What's his interest?"

"He's president of Washbridge Dog Rescue. Edna Vicars had promised to leave some money to them in her Will."

"Did she?"

"No. It went to the kids."

"He thinks they had something to do with her death?"

"Something like that."
"Any proof?"
I shook my head.
"Sounds like a wild goose chase."
"Probably."
"Knock yourself out, but let me know if you find anything."
"Okay, thanks."
"There is one condition though," he said.
"What's that?"
"There's a bowling competition tonight. It's a police thing. Someone has dropped out, and we need a substitute. How about it?"
"Me? I've only bowled once in my life, and I ended up in A&E with my finger stuck in the hole."
"Don't worry. It's only a bit of fun. No one takes it seriously."
I hated bowling, but I didn't want to jeopardise our new working relationship. "Okay, but don't blame me if I'm useless."

Mrs Vicars' neighbour obviously didn't share her passion for gardening. Mrs Vicars' lawn had been recently cut. The flower borders were a kaleidoscope of colours—not a weed to be seen. Next door, by contrast, was a wilderness. The garden had long since succumbed to weeds. An old fridge stood next to the broken fence.

I pressed the doorbell, but didn't hear it ring. It was probably broken. I waited—just in case, but nothing. I knocked quietly at first, and then progressively louder until I became convinced there was no one in. I was halfway down the path when the door opened.

"Mrs Draycott?" I said.

"What?" The old lady had her cardigan on inside out. Her long grey hair was so thin I could see her scalp.

I walked back to the door. "Are you Mrs Draycott?"

"Who are you?"

"My name is Jill Gooder. Detective Jack Maxwell gave me your name."

"Jack and Jill. I loved that nursery rhyme when I was a child."

You and everyone else apparently.

"Could I speak to you about the hit and run?"

"What rum?"

"No, not—could we go inside?" I pointed.

"Why don't you come inside? I'll make us a nice cup of tea."

To my surprise and relief, the interior of the house was spotless. I studied the row of family photographs on the mantelpiece while I waited for her to make the tea.

"Your children?"

"Andrew and Amelia. They've got grown-up kids of their own now," she said, with pride. "I'll soon be a great-grandma."

"Did you know the Vicars' kids?"

"They used to play with mine. They were nice kids, but that Hector—turned into a bad 'un. Biscuit?"

"No thanks."

"I've got all kinds: custard creams, ginger nuts, chocolate digestives—"

All mixed together on the same plate.

"No, thanks. I'm watching my weight."

"You young women. Always on a diet."

"You were telling me about Hector."

"Hardly ever came around to see his mum, and when he did there'd always be an argument."

"What about his sister?"

"Hilary was okay. She used to come around regular like, although I hadn't seen her for a while before—you know."

"Would you mind telling me what happened that day?"

"Poor Edna."

I took a sip of tea while I waited until Mrs Draycott had composed herself.

"I was around the back—taking out the rubbish. There was a horrible noise. Scared me to death it did."

"You didn't actually see it happen then?"

"No, thank goodness. When I got around the front, poor Edna was lying on the road. It was a good job Doctor Mills was there. Not sure what I'd have done otherwise. I was shaking like a leaf."

"The police told me you saw the car."

"There was only one car on the road. Don't know what kind, but it was blue, and it was driving away towards the centre of town."

"Is there anything else you remember? Anything at all?"

"It was that son of hers who did it."

"Hector? What makes you say that? Did you see him?"

"No, but Edna said his name."

"Mrs Vicars was still alive?"

"Only for a few seconds. I told her not to try to speak, but she said, 'Hector, Hector'."

"That's when Doctor Mills turned up. I was real glad to see him."

"How did he get there so quickly? Had he been driving past?"

"No. He was Edna's doctor. She had angina you know."
"Is that all she said? Hector?"
"Yeah. Seconds later she was gone."
"Did you tell the police what she said?"
"I think so. I'm not sure. I was a bit upset. I told 'em about the car."

On my way back to the office, I passed Grandma's new shop again.

Grandma tapped on the window, and beckoned me inside.

"What do you think?"

The shelves were now all full to bursting with yarn. Behind Grandma, the two young assistants smiled nervously. Poor things—imagine working for Grandma—there wasn't a salary high enough.

"It's fantastic. How did you do it so quickly?"

"I have my methods." She turned to her assistants. "Don't just stand there looking gormless. There's plenty of work to do in the back."

The two young women didn't need telling twice. They were probably pleased to get away from her—who could blame them?

"Good staff are so hard to come by," Grandma said.

"They told me it's the grand opening tomorrow."

"That's right. Everyone is coming. Don't be late."

"Me? I might not be—err—I'm—err—really busy."

She glared at me.

"But I'm sure I can make time."

"Be here at ten. On the dot."

"Ten. On the dot. Got it." This was my chance. "I imagine you'll want to postpone our lesson this week.

What with the grand opening?"

The moment the words had left my mouth, I knew I'd said the wrong thing.

"I do not postpone lessons, young lady."

"No, I just thought—"

"Did I ask you to think?"

"No, but—"

"Leave the thinking to me. Just make sure you turn up on time. This is your first level two lesson. I'm expecting great things of you."

"Great things?"

"Anything less won't do."

What was I supposed to wear to go bowling? It had to be trousers because there was a strong possibility that I'd end up sailing down the lane, which would be embarrassing enough without giving everyone a view of my undies. In the end, I settled for jeans. My bum looked pretty damn good in them, even if I did say so myself. I added a blue blouse, and I was good to go. First though, I couldn't resist one more trial of the 'listen' spell. This time it worked first time. I quickly filtered through the chatter until I heard a familiar voice. "Ooh, Ivy. Do that again."

I reversed the spell, and hurried out of the flat as quickly as I could. The less I knew about Mr Ivers' love life, the better for all concerned.

"What are you wearing?" I laughed.

Maxwell looked affronted. "What's wrong with it? It's a bona fide bowling shirt."

"Yeah, I can see that."

"I like it."

"Sure, me too." I laughed again. "You don't think the words: 'Strike Baby!' are a little too much?"

He ignored the snipe.

Maxwell's group had essentially taken over the whole bowling alley. Twelve of the eighteen lanes were occupied by the police bowling club. Burglars would have had free rein in Washbridge that night.

"This is Adam," Maxwell said, as he introduced me to a young man who was fighting a losing battle with acne. "He'll be your partner."

"I thought you wanted me to partner you?" I said.

Maxwell grinned. "No. Bill, over there, is my partner. We're playing against you and Adam."

"You and Bill are wearing matching shirts. How nice."

"We're the dream team."

"I bet you are." I walked over and took a seat next to Adam.

"Are you any good?" he asked, picking at a scab.

"Useless. What about you?"

"The same. Maxwell told me he'd sorted out an experienced player to partner me."

"Did he?" I glared at Maxwell who smirked and gave me a thumbs up.

"It's the last game of the season," Adam said. "If Jack and Bill win tonight, they'll win the league."

"What happened to your regular partner?"

"Joe? He has piles."

Nice image. "Was he any good?"

"Not bad. Until his piles started playing up."

I was beginning to get the picture. Maxwell was one win away from the cup. His opposition had lost a man, so he'd put me forward knowing full well that I couldn't play to save my life. He would win the cup and humiliate me all in one. Okay—if that was the way he wanted to play it—game on!

Adam was the first to bowl. I was no expert, but his style—and I use the term loosely—left much to be desired. He took a huge run at the lane, but then skidded to a halt, and delivered the ball using both hands. The ball meandered at a snail's pace down the lane, ending up in the gutter two feet short of the pins. Maxwell and his partner in crime guffawed with laughter. Adam's second attempt was a little better—taking out three pins.

Bill was next up. He had the air of a pro, and his technique was smooth and aggressive. The ball spun down the lane making contact with the kingpin. The pins flew in all directions leaving a solitary pin on the far left side. Moments later, he mopped up the remaining pin to whoops of 'Spare' from Jack Maxwell.

"What's a spare?" I whispered to Adam.

"It's when you take out all the pins in the two attempts."

It was my turn. I tried to copy what I'd seen Bill do, but my legs got in a twist, and I was lucky to keep my balance. The ball went straight from my hand into the gutter. My second attempt was a repeat performance—in the opposite gutter. Again I could hear Maxwell laughing, but I didn't give him the satisfaction of making eye contact.

Maxwell scored a strike and punched the air.

As soon as Adam released the ball, I cast the spell. The ball which had been headed for the gutter, slowly spun back towards the centre of the lane, gathered momentum, and hit the kingpin full on. Strike! Adam stared open-mouthed. Maxwell and Bill did the same.

"Go Adam!" I shouted.

Adam turned to me — his face a picture, as I gave him a high-five.

Bill's technique was flawless. The bowl spun towards the king pin once again, but this time it seemed to overshoot, and took out only the pin on the far right hand side. For the longest moment, he stared at the pins in disbelief. His second attempt wasn't much better. Just when it appeared it might give him another spare, it veered to the left and missed altogether.

I wonder how that could have happened. Snigger.

With my next two attempts, I earned us a spare while Maxwell drew a blank on both attempts. *How strange.* By the final frame, Adam was really enjoying himself. His score of one-hundred and sixty was a personal best. I'd deliberately kept my own score a little more modest. Maxwell and Bill were livid. Neither of them could understand what had happened to the form that had put them within reach of winning the league. It was the last frame, and with only Maxwell and me left to bowl, the scores were tied.

I picked up the ball, smiled at Maxwell, and made the perfect delivery which gave me my first strike of the evening. I turned to him, grinned, and said, "How's that for a strike, *baby*?"

He wasn't amused. He was even less amused when I scored two more strikes with my final two bowls. Adam was dancing and jumping around like a man possessed. Maxwell and Bill looked like rabbits caught in the headlights.

"Good luck," I said to Maxwell as I returned to my seat.

The game, the league title and the cup rested on Maxwell's next attempt. I was about to cast another spell when I thought better of it. I'd give him a chance. Win or lose now—it was up to him. He stood perfectly still for what felt like an age, and then delivered the ball. All eyes were on it as it careered down the lane. It started out on the right, but then the spin took hold and it moved towards the kingpin. The pins flew in all directions.

All except for one.

"We won!" Adam grabbed me around the waist and spun me around. It seemed like the whole of the bowling alley erupted in applause.

Bill stormed off. Maxwell looked at me, and smiled.

"I suppose I deserved that," he said, once we were outside.

"I suppose you did."

"I've never played so badly." He shook his head.

"I guess the pressure got to you."

"I guess so. I thought you couldn't play. Where did those three strikes come from at the end?"

"I've told you before. I can do magic."

# Chapter 6

"Another two are missing!" Mrs V said, as soon as I walked into the office.

"Another two what?"

"Scarves. This is getting beyond a joke. Did you tell Detective Maxwell?"

"Of course."

"Did he say he'd put out an APB?"

"Something like that."

Mrs V sighed. I'm not sure she believed me. "And there's another one of these parcels." She handed me the offending article.

"Cat treats? Why do they keep sending these?"

Winky was waiting for me. "Did I hear treats mentioned?"

He may have been deficient in the eye department, but there was nothing wrong with his hearing. "You'll get fat."

"We all have our cross to bear. The old bag lady out there is ugly, you're OCD and I'm a little overweight."

"I am not OCD."

"And *I'm* not a talking cat. Now hand over the treats."

There wasn't time to argue. My accountant, Mr Robert Roberts, was due at any moment. When we'd first met, I'd thought the name was a joke. Who, with the surname of Roberts, would name their son Robert? Cruel parents you might think, but you'd be wrong. Mr Robert Roberts was christened James Roberts, but had changed his name by deed poll. True story.

"Good morning, Ms Gooder," Robert Roberts said.

"Good morning, Mr Roberts." I'd long since given up on asking him to call me Jill.

"I've been going through your paperwork." He gave me the same look as he always gave me around this time.

"Okay?"

"It really won't do."

"It won't?" I should introduce Robert Roberts to Grandma. Something tells me they'd hit it off.

"It most certainly won't. You can only enter legitimate business expenses to offset profits."

Profits? What were they? Was that supposed to be a joke? It was difficult to tell with Robert Roberts. He would have made a brilliant straight man.

"I thought that's what I'd done."

He sighed the sigh of someone tired of dealing with a moron.

"A linen basket?" He held up a receipt.

"Yes?"

"Why does a private investigator need a linen basket?"

"It's for Mrs V."

He shook his head — none the wiser.

"My PA/receptionist. You met her just now."

"The woman who tried to give me a scarf?"

"That's the one."

"Why does she need a linen basket?"

"Because Winky got into the mail sack."

"Winky?"

I pointed to the ball of fur which was snoring on the window sill.

"A cat?"

I nodded.

"So." Robert Roberts scratched his nose — one of his

many nervous ticks. "Let me see if I have this straight. You bought a linen basket to replace the mail sack to prevent the cat getting to the mail?"

"Close, but no coconut. The linen basket is to stop Winky getting at the wool."

"Wool?"

"Mrs V's wool. She knits. Scarves."

"Have you branched out?"

"How do you mean?"

"In addition to your main business, do you now sell scarves?"

"Scarves? No. That's just something Mrs V does."

"So, a hobby then?"

"I guess so."

"In that case, you can't claim for the linen basket." He ripped the receipt in half. "And this?" He passed me another receipt. "Eye patches. Is this for some kind of disguise when you're following someone?"

"They aren't for me."

"For your receptionist?"

"For the cat."

Winky stirred, and looked up. He was sporting an eye patch in a pleasing shade of green today.

"He's wearing an eye patch!" Robert Roberts exclaimed.

"That's right. That's what I was trying to tell you."

He ripped that receipt in half too.

"So?" I tried to sound upbeat. "What's the verdict over all?"

Robert Roberts studied the figures on his laptop. "Not good."

"But not bad?" Ever the optimist.

"More like terrible."

"Oh."

"The business seems to be lacking one vital ingredient."

"What's that?"

"Paying customers."

"I have four cases on right now."

"How many of those are for paying customers?"

"More than none."

"How many?"

"Precisely or approximately?"

"Precisely."

"One."

I had an appointment to see Hector Vicars, and I was just about to leave the office when Winky stepped in front of me.

"Out of my way," I said. "I'm running late."

"I need a favour."

"What kind of favour?"

"Check the bottom drawer of the filing cabinet," he said.

The parcel in the drawer was addressed to a Mrs Lake in London SE1. "What's this?"

"Would you post it for me?"

Who was Mrs Lake, and why was Winky sending her a parcel? And what was in it? There was no time to ask; I was already running late. "Okay." I grabbed the parcel and hurried out of the door.

It took me less than a minute to work out that Hector Vicars, Mrs Vicars' son, was a complete tool. He showed me into a room that he insisted on referring to as his 'trophy room'. In fact, it was a small living room with a threadbare sofa, a matching armchair, and a huge TV mounted on the wall. In one corner of the room was a glass fronted cabinet which looked like it had been made from flat-pack. Inside the cabinet were half a dozen trophies interspersed with photographs of Hector, standing next to an assortment of rally cars.

"Do you race, Hector?"

"No one calls me that. Call me Heck."

"Do you race, Heck?"

"I used to."

"Were you any good?"

"What do you think?"

He didn't want to know. "Why did you stop?"

"Retired at the top, didn't I?" His comb-over wasn't working, but his bad breath certainly was.

"When did you last see your mother?"

"Don't remember. A few months ago, maybe."

"Did she ever talk about her Will?"

"Is that what this is all about? Did that stuck-up prat, Briggs, put you up to this?"

"I *am* working for Colonel Briggs."

"He's an idiot. He should be shot along with those stupid dogs of his. He tried to con Mum out of her money."

"I understand your mother was fond of dogs. Wasn't she a judge at the dog shows?"

"Just a stupid hobby."

"What kind of car do you drive?"

"I don't have a car at the moment. No job, so no money for a car."

"Where were you on the day your mother died?"

"How should I know? Shooting probably."

"Shooting?"

"Rabbits, birds, squirrels—"

"So, basically any defenceless creature?"

"Yeah. Do you shoot?"

"No." But I was sorely tempted to start—no prizes for guessing who'd be the target. "Are you sure you didn't drive by your mother's house that day?"

"I told you. I ain't got a car."

"Your mother's next door neighbour told me that your mother said your name just before she died."

"Old Ma Draycott? She's not the full shilling."

"So you weren't there?"

"Told you that already, didn't I?"

"Did your mother ever mention changing her Will in favour of the dog charity?"

"Never. She said she was going to leave it to me and Hills, and that's what she did."

Another wave of bad breath wafted my way—my cue to leave.

If Mrs Vicars *had* cut her son out of her Will, no one would have blamed her.

The so-called 'Action Committee' was everything I'd expected it to be—and less. Peter had stayed at home with the kids, who were still reeling from the news that their long anticipated holiday had been cancelled. According to Kathy, Mikey had taken it particularly badly.

"Who's in charge?" I asked Kathy.

"Dominic Whitelaw. That's him over there." She pointed to the front of the room.

"The guy in the luminous pink shirt?"

"No." She laughed. "That's Gerald. Dominic is standing behind him."

"The short guy?"

"Don't let him hear you say that. He's a bit sensitive about his height."

"Who put him in charge?"

"He appointed himself."

"Nice to see the democratic process is alive and well in Washbridge."

"To be fair, no one else wanted to do it. Dominic used to be a bigwig at the power station. Some kind of senior manager, I think. He's been overseeing its closure. He's used to organising and public speaking."

"Okay, everyone!" Dominic called the meeting to order. "Before we start, I thought we'd agreed that we'd restrict all of our meetings to those involved in the loss." He stared pointedly at me. Before I could speak, Kathy was on her feet. "This is my sister, Jill. She's a private investigator. Some of you probably already know of her through the work she did on the 'Animal' serial killer case."

There were several nods around the room.

"I'm sure your sister is an excellent private investigator," Dominic said. "But our best hope of recovering the money lies with the police. I saw the article in the Bugle. It doesn't appear your sister has the best of working relationships with the constabulary."

"Can I say something?" I got to my feet.

"I'm afraid not," Dominic interrupted. "As I've already said, these meetings are restricted to those directly affected. We'd rather allow the police to do their job. I'm going to have to ask you to leave."

"Hold on a minute!" Kathy said.

"It's okay." I took her hand. "I'll go to your place. You

can fill me in when you get back."

Dominic shot me a smirk masquerading as a smile.

"You're back early." Peter greeted me at the door. "Where's Kathy?"

"The meeting is still going on. The head of the committee didn't want any outsiders there, and he certainly didn't want *me* there."

"Dominic Whitelaw? The man's a pretentious ass."

The kids were still up. Both of them were much more subdued than usual.

"We can't go on holiday," Lizzie said, clutching bion to her chest.

"A bad man stole the money," Mikey said.

"I know. It's really horrible. I'm sorry."

"It isn't your fault," Lizzie said. Bless. I almost cried.

"I know." I forced a smile. "Do you still like magic, Mikey?"

"Yeah! Mum says I can have a magic set for Christmas."

"What about you, Lizzie?"

"I like clowns better."

Really? That was just plain wrong.

"I tell you what, kids. I know a magic trick. Why don't we go into Mikey's bedroom, and I'll show you."

"Don't I get to watch?" Peter pouted.

"Sorry. This is for kids only. No grown-ups allowed."

Mikey led the way. Lizzie and me followed

"What kind of magic can you do?" Lizzie asked.

"Are you a magician?" Mikey shuffled closer to me.

"No. I'm a witch."

Lizzie shuddered. "I don't like witches. They scare me."

"You're a baby." Mikey teased his sister.

"I'm not a wicked witch. I'm a good witch. Good witches aren't scary. You aren't scared of me are you Lizzie?"

She shook her head, but still looked a little unsure. She hadn't completely forgiven me for the Lego hotel incident.

"Which is your favourite car?" I asked Mikey.

He looked at the rows of model cars which were on the shelf above his bed.

"The Ferrari."

"Go and get it for me, then."

Mikey scrambled onto the bed, grabbed the Ferrari and passed it to me.

I placed the model car on the floor in front of me, and said, "Are you ready?"

"What are you going to do, Auntie Jill?" Lizzie asked.

"I'm going to make it disappear."

"You won't lose it will you?" Mikey sounded worried.

"Of course not. It's only a magic trick. Are you both ready?"

They nodded.

"I can't hear you."

"Yes!" they both shouted.

I cast the 'hide' spell, and the car disappeared from view.

"Wow!" Mikey shouted.

"Where's it gone?" Lizzie asked.

I glanced to my right at the full length mirror on the front of the wardrobe. In the reflection I could see the car was still there on the carpet in front of me. "Shall I make it come back?"

They both nodded.

I reversed the spell, and the car reappeared.

"Can you show me how to do that?" Mikey asked.

Whoops! I should have anticipated that.

"It's a witch's secret. Witches aren't allowed to tell."

"Aah." Mikey's face fell.

"You'll be able to do lots of tricks like that one when you get your magic set at Christmas."

"Will you help me?"

"Of course."

"Show us another trick," Mikey said.

"What are you lot up to?" Kathy walked into the bedroom.

"Auntie Jill's a witch," Lizzie shouted.

"She can do magic," Mikey said.

Kathy looked at me. I shrugged.

"Auntie Jill and I need to talk now. Go and play with your dad for a while."

When they'd left, Kathy said, "What was that all about?"

"I was trying to take their minds off the holiday."

"Since when did you do magic tricks?"

"Just some sleight of hand. Something an ex-boyfriend once showed me. I was trying to cheer them up. Anyway, what happened after I left? It can't have gone on for long."

"It didn't. Total waste of time. Dominic just said it was in the hands of the police now, so all we can do is wait."

"We'll see about that."

# Chapter 7

"Morning, Mrs V. You're looking rather splendid this morning."

"Why thank you, dear. Thought I should make the effort for the grand opening of your grandmother's shop."

I should have realised that Grandma would have invited Mrs V too. Winky would just have to man the office while we were both out.

"You don't think the tiara is too much?" She pointed to her head, just in case I wasn't sure where it was.

"Not at all." For the red carpet at a movie première. "It matches your silver choker nicely."

Two-faced? Who? Me?

"Are you going home to get changed before the opening?" She glanced at my ensemble.

"I thought I'd go like this."

"Really? In that top?"

Nothing wrong with a green blouse.

"And those trousers?"

Grey slacks never go out of fashion.

"I think I look okay."

"Yes, well." She sighed.

Never before had two words conveyed so much disapproval.

"I posted your parcel," she said, adjusting her tiara.

"Parcel?"

"The one you left on my desk."

"Right. Thanks."

Winky was on my desk, staring at the computer screen. He didn't bother to look up when I walked in.

"What's going on with these parcels?" I demanded.

"Shush, I'm busy."

I had to hand it to him; the way he manoeuvred the mouse with his paw was impressive. But then: cat - mouse. Made sense I guessed.

"Don't shush me. That's my computer."

"I won't be a minute. Pour me some milk while you're waiting."

Enough already. Who was the boss around here? Don't answer that.

I walked up behind him, and looked at the screen. "Oh, no!"

"What?"

"Tell me you aren't selling Mrs V's scarves."

"I'm not selling Mrs V's scarves."

"Are you?"

"Yes. Surprisingly, they fetch a pretty penny."

"You can't do that!"

"I can. It's actually surprisingly easy. The only difficult part is getting the parcel to the post."

"That's not what I meant. They aren't yours to sell. And besides, you're a cat."

"Your point is?"

"What do you do with the money—" The penny dropped. "You ordered those treats, didn't you?"

"What else am I going to spend it on?"

I snatched the mouse away from him, and shut down the computer. "No more. You can't go around stealing other people's property and selling it."

"Why not?"

"It's called theft."

"She has thousands of scarves. I'm doing her a favour."

"No!"
"What if I split the profits with her fifty fifty?"
"No!"
"Sixty forty?"

I'd no sooner turned onto the high street than I saw them.

The man-sized ball of wool handed me a flyer with the headline *'Grand opening today!'*

All along the street, on both sides, were people dressed as balls of wool - each one a different colour. It must have cost Grandma a small fortune, but that presupposed that she'd actually paid them. Maybe they were all under a mind control spell. Nah, she wouldn't do something like that. Who was I kidding? Of course she would.

The glossy, full colour flyer had a photo of the new shop. At least Grandma had had the sense not to include a photo of herself—that would have scared everyone off.

The shop was full—the flyers had apparently done their job. That, plus the champagne which was flowing freely. I declined the offer of a drink, and made my way through the crowd in search of Grandma.

I found her deep in conversation with Mrs V and two other women who were also sporting tiaras. All of them looked me up and down disapprovingly.

"This is Jill, my granddaughter. As you can see, she's made a real effort today."

Mrs V mouthed, "Told you so."

"Nice promotion," I said by way of a diversion. "All you need now is a brass band."

The words were no sooner out of my mouth than I heard the trombones and trumpets begin to play. Where was that champagne? I needed a drink. My pockets were full of discount vouchers which the man-sized balls of wool had been distributing liberally. The crowds kept on coming. After an hour, I was all yarned out. Grandma was at the rear of the shop with the blue rinse brigade, so I took my chance. Freedom!

"Sneaking away already?" Grandma said.

"No. I—it's—I have an appointment."

"Don't forget you have a lesson later. I expect you to be there on time."

"No problem. I'll be there. Congratulations again on the opening."

I really did have an appointment, although I doubted Grandma believed me. Hilary Vicars was not at all what I'd expected her to be. After my meeting with her obnoxious sibling, I'd feared the worst. In fact, Hilary was polite, unassuming, and more importantly—she didn't have bad breath. Her boyfriend, Battery, though was another matter entirely.

"Could we speak in private?" I asked.

"Hills wants me here," Battery said.

I know what you're thinking—Battery? Her boyfriend obviously hadn't earned the nickname because he was full of energy—Battery was a huge lump of lard. Maybe his nickname was short for 'assault and battery'. He had thug written all over him—no really—he actually did have 'thug' tattooed on the fingers of each hand. Classy.

"I'm sure Hilary can speak for herself," I said.

Hilary turned to her boyfriend who shook his head. At least I think he did—he had such a thick neck it was difficult for him to move his head at all.

"I'd like Battery to stay," Hilary said without making eye contact with me.

"Okay. I want to ask you a few questions about your mother, if that's all right?"

She nodded, but still didn't make eye contact.

"Did she ever mention changing her Will?"

"Yes."

"She did? What did she say exactly?"

"She said she was going to leave some money to Washbridge Dog Rescue."

"How did you feel about that?"

Hilary shrugged.

"You must have had some feelings about it. It was money you'd probably expected to inherit."

"I don't really like dogs. One bit me when I was little."

"So you didn't like the idea of your mother leaving her money to them?"

Hilary shook her head. I couldn't fault her honesty.

"When did you last see your mother?"

"A few days before she died." Tears welled in her eyes as she spoke.

"Did she say anything about the Will then?"

"No. We talked about her garden mainly. She was very proud of it."

"How was she? Health wise?"

"She had angina, but other than that, she was okay. She had regular check ups at the surgery. She said home visits were for old people." Hilary managed a weak smile at the memory.

"That's enough questions." Battery stepped forward.

"Just one more thing. What kind of car do you drive?"

"I don't. It was stolen—"

"That's it!" Battery took hold of my arm. I toyed with the idea of casting the 'power' spell, so I could throw him across the room, but I thought better of it.

"Mrs V, do you remember the name of that guy my dad used to use to trace cars?"

"You mean Seamus-the-wheel?"

"That's him."

I found his number on Dad's old Rolodex and gave him a call.

"Hello?" he said. I loved that Irish accent.

"Seamus?"

"Who's that?"

"Seamus, it's Jill Gooder, Ken's daughter."

"Jill. How are you darlin'? It's been ages and a day."

"I'm okay, thanks. How about you?"

"I keep going, you know. As long as there's Guinness, I'll be okay. What can I be doing for you?"

"I was wondering. Do you still do the cars?"

Seamus-the-wheel knew everything there was to know about cars, but his speciality was in finding them. He worked both sides of the law. If you needed a particular car stealing, he'd find it. If you'd had a car stolen, he'd find it. His methods were a black box, and it was understood that no questions would be asked. Dad had used Seamus on several occasions, and he'd always delivered.

"I'm mostly retired, but I still keep my hand in for a few old friends."

"Would you be able to help me?"

"You shouldn't need to ask, darlin'. Anything for Ken Gooder's daughter. What can I do you for?"

I gave him the names and addresses of Hector and Hilary Vicars, and asked if he could check on any cars that the siblings owned, or may have owned in the recent past. He promised to have something for me within a few days.

Kathy had arranged for me to talk to Natasha Cutts, the girlfriend of Norman Reeves, the holiday fund organiser who had disappeared along with the cash. Natasha made me look tall; she barely came up to my chin.

"Hi." She seemed to have the weight of the world on her shoulders. "Come in."

"Thanks."

We went through to her living room. Every surface was covered with thimbles.

"You collect thimbles." Nothing like stating the obvious.

I wondered if she had them catalogued—I was guessing she did.

"Since I was six."

"Nice." I'd just about exhausted my thimble-related conversation. "Do you knit?" Perhaps a discount voucher for Grandma's shop might cheer her up.

"Knit? No. Why?"

"No reason." I pushed the vouchers back into my pocket.

"Everyone blames me." She began to cry.

I checked my pockets for a tissue, but could find only discount vouchers.

"I haven't heard anyone blame you," I lied. I'd actually heard plenty of people sticking the boot in during my brief attendance at the action committee meeting. Guilt by association as far as they were concerned.

"How long have you been with Norman?"

"Not long." She sniffed. "Only a few weeks."

"Had he been acting strangely at all?"

She shook her head.

"Did he have money problems?"

"Not as far as I know, but then we never really discussed money." She stood up. "Do you mind if I make a cup of tea?"

"Sure. Go ahead."

"Would you like one?"

"Please. Milk and one and two-thirds spoonfuls of sugar."

I followed her into the kitchen where she put on the kettle, then blew her nose. "Sorry about this. It's all getting a bit too much. Would you like a biscuit?"

She offered me the biscuit tin, and I was about to refuse when I spotted that it was full of custard creams—and only custard creams!

"Don't mind if I do."

"Take two."

I slipped the third one back into the tin. "Thanks."

By the time she was on her second biscuit, she'd come around a little. "Norman seemed like a good guy, you know."

"When was the last time you saw him?"

"We went to that little Italian restaurant. Antonio's it's called."

"I can't say I know it."

"It's out of town. The food was great, but the service was a little slow."

"Did he seem okay? Did he say or do anything out of the ordinary?"

"Nothing. It was a lovely evening."

"Did you go home with him afterwards?" Subtle—that's me.

"No. We both had work the next day, and we'd been drinking, so we took separate cabs."

"Do you have a recent photo of him?"

"Only on here." She picked up her phone, scrolled through the menu, and then held it out for me to see.

The tall, gangly young man was obviously camera-shy.

"Could you email that to me?"

"Sure."

I asked a few more questions, and then took my leave—taking particular care to avoid any thimble-related accidents on the way out.

There was no sign of Mrs V when I got back to the office—no doubt still enjoying the free champagne with the other yarnies (woollies)? She'd left another delivery of cat treats on my desk.

"I believe these belong to you?" I held out the packet of treats.

"Gimme, gimme, gimme." Winky weaved through my legs.

"This is the last time. Got it? No more selling Mrs V's scarves."

Winky shrugged.

"If you do, I'll tell her you're responsible for the missing scarves, and there's no guessing what she might do. It's a long way down from that window."

"Okay, okay. Just give me those."

Did I trust him? Not as far as I could throw him. But the threat of Mrs V taking her revenge might be enough to curtail his scarf thievery.

Holy moly. I'd lost track of time. My lesson with Grandma was scheduled to start in ten minutes. Maybe she'd be so drunk that she'd forget. Some chance. I had to get there, and get there fast. Whenever possible, I still liked to take the car to Candlefield. The journey along quiet roads, through beautiful scenery, was a great way to shake off the tensions of the day. Luckily I had a backup plan. I could use the level three spell which Grandma had shown me when I'd been stuck in Candlefield without my car. It wasn't an easy spell—it could be exhausting—but right now it was Hobson's choice.

I hadn't yet mastered the landing, and once again landed on my backside with a thud.

"That had to hurt," Amber said.

"What level is that spell?" Pearl asked.

The twins had been waiting outside Grandma's house when I landed, unceremoniously in front of them.

"Level three." I picked myself up—trying to resist the urge to rub my sore bottom.

"Wow!" Amber said. "You really are leaving us behind."

The twins had been stuck on level two for some years. The last thing I wanted to do was to make them feel bad.

"Not really. This is my first level two lesson today. I'm going to need your help."

"Why are you three waiting out here?" Grandma appeared in the doorway. "Come on in. We have lots to get through."

We followed her inside.

"And Jill, brush your trousers down. You have gravel

on your backside."

# Chapter 8

"Grandma's new shop, Ever A Wool Moment, opened today," I told the twins in a voice loud enough for Grandma to hear. "It was a great success." What? I'm not above a little sucking up.

"When do we get to see it?" Amber asked.

Grandma was stony-faced. "Why are you discussing my shop?"

Whoops.

"I just wanted to tell the twins how well the opening went."

"Is this the right time?"

I could tell from her expression that the answer wasn't 'yes'. "Sorry."

"You all need to pay attention," Grandma said. "You two." She pointed to the twins. "You have been stuck on level two for too long. It doesn't reflect well on me."

Amber and Pearl both studied their feet.

"And you." Grandma turned to face me. "No more gossiping about yarn. Understand?"

"Got it. Sorry."

There was only one spell on the agenda today. Grandma had said that one level two spell per lesson was enough. No arguments from me there. Today's spell was 'listen' which had been responsible for introducing me to Mr Ivers' mysterious love life.

"I hate this spell," Amber whispered to me.

"Me too," Pearl said.

"As I've told the girls a million times," Grandma said. "Level one spells are easy. From level two onwards it's all about focus. Any idiot can memorise a spell."

The twins exchanged a glance.

"At least that's what I used to think." She glared at Amber and Pearl. "These two appear to be the exception to the rule. Maybe you'll be able to drag them up with you, Jill."

I felt terrible. The last thing I wanted to do was embarrass my cousins. "I'm sure we can all help one another."

The twins managed a smile. Grandma didn't.

She left the three of us alone for ten minutes to give us time to prepare.

"I always make a mess of this one," Amber said, desperately studying the book.

"I've never managed it yet." Pearl was looking over her sister's shoulder.

"Do you remember the images?" I asked.

"Yeah, I think so," Pearl said. "I've tried it so many times that I know them off by heart."

"Me too." Amber nodded.

"Then forget the book. It isn't going to tell you anything you don't already know. I tried this spell at home, and I couldn't get it to work either, but then my mother appeared and told me what I'd been doing wrong. It's like Grandma says, it's all in the focus; it's all about the concentration."

"I'm afraid I'll forget the images or mix them up," Amber said.

"That's the problem right there. Instead of focussing on casting the spell, you're worrying about remembering the images, but they're already in your memory. Just focus your mind on the desired result. Nothing else."

The twins looked at me, and then at one another. They

weren't exactly exuding confidence.

"Time's up." Grandma had rejoined us. "We need to go outside for this."

The three of us followed her. I noticed the twins were holding hands.

"Jill," Grandma said. "You can go first. Do you see those two women at the bottom of the hill?"

I nodded. The two women in question were deep in conversation. The younger one of the two had a pram. The older one was staring down into the pram.

"I want you to tell me what they're saying."

Wasn't eavesdropping rather rude? Not if Grandma ordered you to do it.

I closed my eyes, and remembered what my mother had told me. Focus. Concentrate. This time the blast of noise didn't come as such a shock, and I was able to quickly filter out all sounds except the conversation between the two women.

"The older one said that the baby reminded her of her son when he was a baby. The younger one said she hasn't had a good night's sleep since he was born."

"Very good," Grandma said. "Amber, you can go next."

Amber released her sister's hand, and stepped forward. She looked terrified. I felt so sorry for her.

Grandma looked up the hill this time. "See those two young boys. Tell me what they're saying."

Amber looked at me, and I mouthed the word 'focus'.

She nodded and closed her eyes. I studied her expression as she began to cast the spell. After only a few seconds, she smiled a huge smile.

"The one on the bike said that he's going to the park.

The other boy said he isn't allowed to go because he didn't do his homework."

"Well done, Amber," Grandma said. "Not before time."

Pearl looked even more nervous than her sister had done. After Amber's success, the pressure on her was even greater.

"Focus," Amber said. "It really works."

Pearl tried to smile, but looked close to tears.

"Do you see the man and woman up there, on the opposite side of the road to the two young boys?"

Pearl nodded.

"Tell me what they're saying."

I had everything crossed. Amber did too by the look of it. Although the twins spent most of their waking hours squabbling, they obviously cared deeply for one another.

Pearl closed her eyes; the concentration was etched on her face.

"He asked her what's for dinner. She said whatever he makes."

Amber embraced her sister. I embraced them both.

"The cupcakes are on us!" Pearl said, as we walked up the hill.

The lesson was over, and Grandma had declared herself satisfied with our performance. True praise indeed from her.

"Thanks, Jill." Amber gave my hand a squeeze. The twins were walking either side of me.

"I didn't do anything. It was down to you."

"We couldn't have done it without you." Pearl squeezed my other hand. "Goodness knows we've tried often enough."

I was pleased to have helped them, but was still a little embarrassed. I was acutely aware that I was still very much the newbie. The twins had been witches since the day they were born. But then, I guess I had too—I simply hadn't known it.

"You're going to be a great witch," Amber said. "Just like Grandma."

Pearl and I both stopped and looked at her.

"Sorry. I didn't mean *just* like Grandma. You're way too pretty, and kind. When I said—"

"Keep digging." Pearl teased her sister.

"You know what I mean. You're going to be a level six witch. And at the rate you're progressing, it won't take long."

"She's right," Pearl said. "We've grown up with lots of witches, and hardly any of them have advanced beyond level four. None of them have made it all the way to level six, but you will."

I was overwhelmed, but knew I had to keep my feet on the ground. Much as I loved my cousins, and appreciated their kind words, I wasn't sure they were the best judge of my abilities or potential. Grandma would probably have had a different take on it.

It took me a while to track down Antonio's Italian Restaurant. Hardly surprising as it was in the back end of nowhere. The food must have been exceptional. Why else would anyone have travelled all that way when there were more Italian restaurants in Washbridge city centre than you could shake a pizza at?

As always, I tried the formal, official approach first. I asked the manager if I could view his CCTV.

'Need a warrant blah, blah, blah.'
'Data protection blah, blah, blah.'
'You're not the police blah, blah, blah.'

No one could say I hadn't tried, but now it was time for plan B. Invisibility really was a witch's best friend.

It took me a while to track down the room where the CCTV monitors were located, so I was forced to hide in a broom cupboard for thirty minutes in between periods of invisibility. The restaurant was empty because it wasn't due to open for a couple of hours, and most of the staff were in the kitchen. The CCTV monitors were in an office which was only slightly larger than the broom cupboard. The door was unlocked — security was all very low key.

The on-screen menu listed the CCTV recordings by date. Two clicks with the mouse, and I was viewing footage from the night in question. There were only two cameras. One focussed on the bar; the other on the pay desk. That made sense because if anyone was going to try to rob the place, those would be the likeliest targets. Despite its out of town location, Antonio's was obviously popular. On-screen a steady stream of customers could be seen walking by the pay desk on their way in and out of the restaurant. At around the eight-fifteen mark, I saw Natasha Cutts walk in. The man at her side had his back to the camera. Two hours later, they reappeared, the man waited for her at the door while she paid the bill using plastic. I still couldn't get a good look at Norman Reeves who, on this evidence, was a cheapskate who allowed his date to pick up the bill.

When I got back to my flat, I gave Kathy a call to update her.

"Not much to report so far," I said. "I've spoken to Natasha. She was pretty upset. She thinks everyone blames her."

"She shouldn't take any notice. Most people know it's not her fault. There are always a few loudmouths willing to throw accusations around."

"I've checked the CCTV at the restaurant where they ate. That was the last time she saw him."

"How did you manage to view the CCTV?"

"If I told you that, I'd be forced to kill you."

"Don't go getting yourself in hot water with the police again. Not now you and Jacky boy are on such good terms."

"What have I told you about calling him Jacky boy?"

"You and he have made up though, haven't you?"

"For now, I guess. Although I still haven't forgiven him for trying to make me look a fool at the bowling alley."

"You didn't tell me about that."

"It was nothing. He asked me to make up the numbers for some police league thing."

"You? Ten-pin bowling? That's a laugh."

"That's what he thought until I handed his ass to him."

# Chapter 9

It took Kathy a couple of minutes to stop laughing. Why did she find the idea of me winning at bowling so hard to believe?

"How are the kids?" I asked.

"They keep asking when Auntie Jill the witch is going to give them a repeat performance. I think you may have started something there."

"I only know the one trick."

"You'd better get swotting up on card tricks then or you'll have some disappointed kids on your hands. Speaking of which, I've had a brilliant idea."

Two words I'd hoped never to hear from Kathy's lips were: brilliant and idea. Her ideas were rarely brilliant, in fact most of the time they struggled to be mediocre. More worryingly, they invariably involved me.

"Aren't you going to ask me what it is?" she said.

I didn't want to know. I really didn't want to know. "What is it?" I just had to ask, didn't I?

"I was thinking. After all the disappointment of the holiday cancellation, we could take the kids to Candlefield. If you can find your way there, that is." She laughed.

"Candlefield?" I wasn't laughing.

"You remember. The land that SatNav forgot. From how you described it, the kids will love it. Do you think your family will be able to put us up? Or is there a cheap B&B?"

Did the 'forget' spell work over the phone? I tried it—it failed miserably.

"What do you think?" Kathy asked. "Brilliant idea or

what?"

"Brilliant, yeah. Have you mentioned this to Peter and the kids?"

"Yes. We were talking about it all of last night. Pete's up for it and the kids can't wait."

"Great."

"When could we arrange it? It would be fantastic if we could do it on the same dates as the holiday had been planned for."

"I'll have to talk to Aunt Lucy and Grandma. I'll see what they say. I'd better get going—criminals to catch and all that."

Mrs V was AWOL when I arrived at the office the next morning. It wasn't that long since she'd had a spell in hospital. I hoped she hadn't had some kind of relapse.

"Have you seen Mrs—?" I stopped dead in my tracks. "Winky, what are you doing?"

"What does it look like?"

"It looks like you're waving two tiny flags around."

"They aren't that tiny."

Because obviously it was the *size* of the flags that was the point at issue here.

"Okay, why are you waving those average size flags around?"

He was sitting on the window sill, and had yet to look at me.

"How do you spell 'cutie'? Is it a 'Y' or 'I E' at the end?" he asked.

"I E, I think. Never mind that. Why are you waving them around?"

Winky sighed—obviously annoyed by the interruption.

"I am not 'waving flags around' as you put it. This is semaphore."

"Sema—"

"phore. Yes. What about rendezvous? How do you spell that?"

I walked up to the window and looked out across the way.

"There's another cat over there with flags," I said.

"Well of course there is. You didn't think I was talking to myself did you? That would be crazy."

Totally. Whereas two cats exchanging messages via semaphore was completely sane.

"Who is she? I assume it's a she?"

"Bella." Winky sighed. He was smitten.

"How long have you and Bella been exchanging semaphore messages?"

"Not long. She wants me to get a phone, so we can text. I'd have got one by now if you hadn't shut down my scarf sale operation."

"Scarf *theft*."

"Whatever."

"Speaking of scarves, have you seen Mrs V?"

"Not today. Missing her already."

"I wonder if she's ill."

"I'm sorry, but you seem to have mistaken me for someone who gives a monkey's. Now, if you'll excuse me, I have sweet nothings to semaphore."

There was a time, not so very long ago when I'd lived in the land of the sane. No witches, no magic spells, and no crazy cats waving flags at their girlfriends. Happy days.

I decided to go and check on Mrs V. As I walked out of

the building, I glanced up. Bella, Winky's new love interest, was still waving her flags around. She appeared quite animated—maybe they were talking dirty to one another—it didn't bear thinking about. I wondered if I should pay a visit to the flat where Bella lived. Did her owners know about their cat's exploits? In the end, I thought better of it. Any conversation which began with the sentence: 'Do you know your cat is sending semaphore messages to my cat?' couldn't end well.

As I drove past 'Ever a Wool Moment' I glanced inside, and spotted Mrs V behind the counter. Parking wasn't allowed anywhere along the road, but there were no wardens in sight, so I decided to take my chances. I'd only be a couple of minutes.

Mrs V was taking a payment from a woman who was stocking up on yellow yarn. I waited until they'd finished.

"Mrs V?"

"Jill! Have you decided to take up knitting?"

"Me? No. I was just wondering what you're doing here."

"Working, dear. It's been incredibly busy. We're almost out of number nines."

I nodded as though I had a clue what that meant. "Aren't you supposed to be working for me?"

"Of course, but your grandma asked if I'd mind standing in for a couple of days. Just until the full-time manager starts."

That was nice of her. Nice to be consulted.

"Good of you to drop by, Jill," Grandma said.

She'd done it again—crept up on me without my hearing. "Grandma. I didn't see you there."

"Obviously."

"Mrs V tells me she's working for you."

"Only for a couple of days. Is that a problem?"

"Problem? No, of course not. No problem at all."

"Good." She glanced out of the window. "You might want to get going. I think you're about to get a ticket."

You have got to be kidding me. "Miss!" I called to the traffic warden who was checking my registration plate. "I'm back. I was only inside for a minute."

She turned to face me.

"Daze?"

"Hi, Jill. Can we take a ride? I need a word."

"Sure, yeah. Jump in."

As we drove away, I glanced at her uniform.

"Do you like it?" She touched the jacket.

"I thought you worked in fast-food. Undercover, I mean."

"I like to change things around. It stops me getting bored, and keeps the Rogues guessing. I'm not sure how long I'll stick with this one though. I've had some real abuse—one guy was lucky I didn't turn him into a slug."

As we pulled up at a red light, I felt eyes burning into me. I glanced over to the car alongside me to see Kathy waving.

I waved back.

"Who's that?" Daze asked. "She looks a bit crazy."

"That's Kathy, my sister. Well, adoptive sister to be precise. She's a human—she doesn't know about—you know."

"Should I wave back?" Daze asked.

"Why not?"

As soon as the lights changed, I sped away. Memo to self: Before I saw Kathy next, I'd need to come up with an explanation for why I'd had a parking warden with me in the car.

I drove out of town, found a quiet lay-by, and pulled over.

"Was that your grandmother in the wool shop?" Daze asked.

"Yeah. It's her latest venture."

"How do you feel about that?"

"I'm not crazy about it. At least before she opened the shop, I could find refuge from her in the human world. Now, she's right down the street and is stealing my staff."

Daze laughed. "Relatives? Who'd have 'em?"

I would. Even though some of my new family were a sandwich short of a picnic, it was still better than having no family.

"I need a favour," Daze said.

This sounded like more unpaid work—Robert Roberts would be thrilled. "What's that?"

"I'm on the trail of a rogue vampire. I've been after him for a while now, but he's smart and keeps giving me the slip."

"What's he done?"

"The usual. Seduced young women, drunk their blood and left them for dead."

And I thought *I'd* been on some lousy dates. "Where do I come in?"

"It just so happens, you're his type."

"Slim, attractive, intelligent and funny?"

"O negative."

I shuddered. "Blood type? You're kidding?"

She wasn't. "I need you to put up a profile on the dating website he frequents."

"What's that? Bloodsuckingmatchmakers.com?"

She laughed. "No, it's just one of the regular dating websites."

"I know they ask for a lot of personal data to help them make a match, but I didn't realise they asked for blood type."

"They don't. He has certain preferences when it comes to appearance—I'll provide you with a photo that will fit the bill. When he meets his victims—err—dates—he can sense their blood type. Those with other blood types get a meal and a goodnight kiss. Those with O negative become *his* meal."

"But he'll realise something is wrong when the photo in my profile doesn't match—this." I framed my face with my hands.

"Not a problem. You can cast a spell that will make him see what he is expecting to see."

"Will the 'doppelganger' spell work—with a vampire I mean? Won't he see right through it?"

"It'll only fool him for a short time, but it should be long enough."

"Not to sound too much of a wimp, but won't it be dangerous?"

"You'll be fine. I'll be close by, and as soon as he makes his move, I'll be on him."

"Makes his move? Care to define that?"

"I have to wait until his fangs are out or the case will be dismissed."

"Let me make sure I have this right. You want me to be the bait. And you can't step in until he's about to sink his teeth into my neck?"

"You've got it. I'll owe you one."

"Let's hope I'll still be around to collect."

I dropped Daze back in the city centre just in time for her to issue a ticket to a woman who'd left her 4x4 in a no parking zone while she had her nails done.

My phone rang. It was the nursing home.

"I'm very sorry. I've checked our records, and your mother didn't actually have any jewellery on her when she passed away."

"That's not right. She was definitely wearing a ring on a necklace. It had been her grandmother's wedding ring."

"Did you see it yourself when you visited her?"

"No." The state I'd been in on that particular day I doubt I'd have noticed if she'd been wearing a top hat. "But, I'm sure she was wearing it."

"Maybe she took it off before coming into the home?"

"No, she was definitely wearing it."

"Not according to our records. I'm sorry I can't be of more help."

Something didn't smell right.

# Chapter 10

I woke early the next morning. I hadn't slept particularly well because my mind had been working overtime trying to figure out what I was going to do about Kathy. The whole thing was such a mess. I wished I'd never mentioned Candlefield to her, but at the time I had no idea of its significance. If it was just Kathy, I'd use the 'forget' spell, but this time Peter and the kids were involved too. I planned to speak to Aunt Lucy and even to Grandma if necessary—that's how desperate I was. Maybe they could come up with some kind of long-term solution. In the meantime, I had to find the missing holiday money, and I had to find it fast.

I flicked through the book of spells. There was a much wider range of spells in level two than there had been in level one, but as Grandma repeatedly emphasised, they also required far more focus. Some of the spells looked downright dangerous. For example, 'fireproof', would allow me to walk through fire unscathed. That was one spell I'd better get right first time otherwise I'd be toast.

One spell in particular caught my eye. The 'ageing' spell would apparently allow me to change my age. When I first spotted it, I'd got all excited. The prospect of losing a few years—even if it did only last for a maximum of twelve hours—had been quite appealing. Then I read the small print. The ageing process only worked in one direction—and it wasn't younger. Bummer.

What would I look like when I was older? Did I really want to know? Call it morbid curiosity, but I did. I read and re-read the description and instructions to be absolutely sure that I knew how to reverse the spell. I was in no hurry to become a permanent member of Mrs V's blue rinse and tiara set. The number of years I aged would depend on the strength of the spell I cast.

I stepped in front of the mirror, closed my eyes and cast the spell. I didn't want to overdo it, so I didn't focus for more than a few seconds. When I opened my eyes, an older version of me was staring back from the mirror. The grey hair was something of a shock, but nothing compared to my face. How old was I? Fifty? Sixty? It was hard to tell. Thank goodness I hadn't focussed on the spell for any longer.

I jumped when my phone rang. Still transfixed by my reflection, I said, "Hello?"

"Jill?"

"Hi."

"Are you okay? You sound—funny."

She was right. Even my voice was different. "I've got a sore throat."

"Are you sure you weren't on the pop last night?"

"What do you want? I have to get to work."

"Okay, Miss Grouchy Pants. Jeez, you're turning into a right old woman."

If only she knew.

"I wondered if you'd had time to talk to your Aunt Lucy about us going over there yet?"

"Not yet, but I will, I promise. Got to go. See you."

"Jill wait—"

I ended the call.

Thank goodness the spell reversal worked first time. I didn't think much to being old, but it had given me an idea.

Mrs V was at her desk, and did not look happy. If that stupid cat had been stealing her scarves again, I'd stick his flags where the sun didn't shine.

"Morning, Jill."

"I thought you were working in Grandma's shop for a few days."

"Don't mention that woman to me."

Oh no.

"Do you know what she did?"

I dare not imagine.

"I'll tell you what she did."

Must you? Blissful ignorance is fine by me.

"She said I needed training."

That didn't sound too bad. It could have been much worse. Toads or slugs could have been involved.

"Training? Can you believe it?" Mrs V continued. "What I don't know about knitting isn't worth knowing."

"What did she say exactly?"

"That I needed to update my skills."

"What did you say?"

"I told her she could stuff her job, and her shop."

"And how did she take it?"

"I didn't stick around to find out. She was still ranting and raving when I left."

"But you're feeling okay?"

"Of course. Never better."

"You're sure?"

"Fit as a fiddle. You know me."

I knew Grandma too. And I knew that crossing her wasn't a smart thing to do.

"You look a little peaky yourself," Mrs V said. "You work too hard. If you aren't careful, this job will age you before your time."

"What do you mean? Do I have a wrinkle?" I ran a finger across my face.

"Of course not. Don't be silly. You're in your prime. I just don't want to see you run yourself into the ground. How about I make us both a drink?"

"Thanks, that would be great."

Mrs V stood up from her desk, and walked across to the coffee machine.

Oh no! No! No! No!

"Where is she?" I screamed at one of the assistants. "Where is she?"

Ever a Wool Moment was much quieter than on 'grand opening' day.

Before the terrified assistant could reply, Grandma appeared from the back office.

"What's all the shouting about? Are you trying to scare away my customers?"

"Change them back!" I screamed.

"Change what back? You aren't making any sense."

"You know what I'm talking about. Mrs V's legs—change them back."

"They look so much better than her own legs. Those varicose veins—yuk."

"You've given her frog's legs."

"Toad's actually. You really must learn to tell the diff—"

"Change them back."

I glanced around and realised that the customers and sales assistants were all staring at us.

"Let's go into the back," I said.

Grandma led the way.

"Change her legs back right now!"

"Relax, she doesn't even know she has them. No human can see them. I don't know what all the fuss is about."

"*I* can see them. How am I meant to work with her when I know she has frog's legs?"

"Toad's."

"Whatever. You have to change them back right now!"

"Or what? If I didn't know better, I'd say you were threatening me."

I was shaking with rage. "If you don't change them back, I'll never come to Candlefield again—and I'll renounce my witchmanship."

"Witchmanship? That isn't even a word."

"You know what I mean. If you don't do it, I'm done with being a witch, and I'm done with you."

My heart was racing. Had I totally lost my mind? This was Grandma I was dealing with. You don't mess with Grandma. Any moment now I could find myself transformed into a rat, or a flea—or mouse droppings.

Grandma's wart was glowing red; that couldn't be a good sign.

"Very well. Just this once, but don't think you can go around threatening me, young lady or you may discover how powerful my magic can be."

"So you'll change her legs back?"

"It's already done."

"Thank you."

"Where did you go?" Mrs V said when I arrived back at the office, breathless. "Your coffee is going cold."

"Sorry. Minor emergency. All sorted now." I tried to see

her legs under the desk.

"What did I say to you about overdoing it?" she said. "If you're not careful, you'll end up old and decrepit like me. When you get to my age, everything starts to wear out." She swung around on the chair, and began to rub her calves. "My legs are giving me gyp today."

"Varicose veins," I said. "You have varicose veins."

"Had them for years, dear. I'm surprised you haven't noticed them before. They're the bane of my life."

"Mrs V, I love your varicose veins."

"You've changed the password," Winky said, as I walked through to my office. He was hammering on the keyboard in frustration.

"That's right."

"How am I supposed to log on?"

"You aren't, that's the whole point. There's to be no more selling stolen scarves, ordering treats or eye patches. The computer is off-limits."

"What about a smartphone then?"

"No computer, no smartphone, tablet or any other device. The digital world is not a place for felines. It's time you went back to being a normal cat."

"I am normal. Are you saying I'm not normal? It's because I have only one eye isn't it? That's discrimination. I could report you."

"It has nothing to do with your eyes—sorry, eye. It's all the other stuff you get up to. You never used to do those things."

"Of course I did. Every cat does. It's just that humans are too stupid to realise. Since you upgraded—"

"Upgraded?"

"Became a witch. Since then, you've been able to see the real me."

"The stealing, computer hacking, semaphore-signalling you."

"Exactly."

"The computer is still out of bounds."

"It's only a matter of time before I crack your password. You're so predictable."

"I am not."

"Jack, Jacky Boy, Maxwell? Am I getting close?"

Damn, I'd have to change it again.

I'd never actually set up a profile on an online dating site before. Daze had sent me the information and photograph that I was to use. The name she'd picked for me was Scarlet Hill—oh dear! The woman in the photo was taller, slimmer and more attractive than me—I hated her, whoever she was. Daze seemed confident that my false profile would attract the rogue vampire. I kind of hoped it wouldn't. The thought of those fangs sinking into my neck brought me out in a cold sweat.

Profile completed, I paid the first month's subscription which made my details available to others, but which also meant I could browse other members' profiles. Just for a laugh, I did a few searches based on my ideal man: breathing, not a cheating scum bag, doesn't pick his nose—that kind of thing. To narrow the results even further, I re-ran the search specifying only members within a fifteen mile radius. The results weren't what I'd expected. I'd assumed that I'd be presented with a gallery of ugly, no-hope losers, but instead the majority looked like normal human beings. Several of the men were quite handsome, and a few were really hot. Which begged the question, why did they need to use an online dating site? Perhaps they had busy lives, and didn't have time to meet women in the conventional way. Or perhaps they were psycho killers. They should include that in the profile questionnaire: 'are you a psycho killer?'

# Chapter 11

It turns out that when you're old you don't need magic to become invisible.

Time was running out to find my mother's ring. Although she hadn't said anything to me herself, I knew from what Alberto had told me, that it would ruin her wedding day if she had to make do with a substitute ring.

The story I'd got from the nursing home didn't ring true (pun intended). My best chance of finding it was to get inside there, and what better way to do it than undercover. I'd slipped through reception using the 'invisible' spell, found a storage cupboard where I could change into some 'old lady' clothes I'd brought with me, and then cast the 'ageing' spell. I'd focussed for longer than on my first attempt, with the result that I now had the face and body of an eighty year old. I also had aches and pains in every joint.

I'd been worried that one of the staff might question who I was, and why I was there. I needn't have worried. The moment I became eighty, I also became part of the furniture. I was able to wander around the building without once being challenged. After twenty minutes, my old bones were ready for a rest. The 'community room' was in the centre of the nursing home. A TV on the wall was showing reruns of a murder mystery series—not that anyone was watching. The residents were mostly asleep in their chairs. One woman was crocheting, another was reading a magazine. Men were in the minority—I'd seen only three so far.

I hobbled over to the patio doors, and lowered myself gently into one of the high-backed chairs. An orderly was doing her rounds with the tea trolley. I took a cup of tea but declined the biscuits which were mixed together on the same plate.

"Hello, sexy," said a voice to my right.

My neck was stiff, so I could only turn my head slowly.

"You're new here, aren't you?" The man, who had taken the seat next to mine, was eighty if he was a day. Toothless, he gave me a gummy smile. "I'm Charlie. Chas to my friends."

"Jill."

"Nice to make your acquaintance, Jill." He put his bony hand on my bony hand. "About time we had some new talent."

Unbelievable! He was coming on to me. My eighty year old self was already getting more action than my younger self ever did.

"Have you been in here long, Chas?" I said.

"Getting on for two years now. Guess there's only one way out for me."

"Don't you have family?"

"Got a son. The boy's a waste of space. He's just waiting to get his hands on my money." He laughed a chesty laugh. "He'll have a long wait. I spent it all on booze, cigars and women. Had one helluva time doing it too."

I bet he had. Good for him. If his son was anything like Hector Vicars, then who could blame him?

"What are the staff like here?" I asked.

"Most of them are okay. The nurses are really good—hot too, some of them." His eyes lit up. "Wouldn't trust some of the others though."

"What do you mean?"

"Just rumours, I suppose."

"What did you hear?"

"You're pretty nosy for a new 'un. Did you used to be a cop or something?"

"Cop? No. I'm a private investigator with special magical powers."

Chas roared with laughter. "Magical powers eh? I could do with some of them magical powers."

I was afraid to ask what he'd use them for. "One of my friends was in here recently."

"What was her name? I know most of the ladies." Another gummy grin.

I just bet he did.

"Darlene Millbright."

"Darlene?" He scratched his chin. "Can't say I remember no Darlene."

"She was very ill when they brought her in. She wouldn't have been here for long before she died."

He nodded—more solemn now.

I continued, "Her daughter told me Darlene had been wearing a ring when she came in, but it had disappeared when they came to bury her. She asked about it, but the staff said her mother hadn't been wearing one."

"Happens a lot."

"It does?"

He looked around to make sure no one could overhear. "That's what I hear. Usually happens where there are no close relatives, so there's no one to notice."

"Someone should tell the police."

"Who's going to listen to a bunch of old codgers? They think because we're old, that we're stupid too."

Chas was definitely not stupid. Frisky, maybe. But not stupid. He'd been in Daleside long enough to know his way around, and to have an idea who might be behind the thefts. I picked his brains for the next hour.

"Time for my afternoon nap," I said, pulling myself to my feet.

"Like some company?" He gummed at me.

"No thanks."

"Maybe another time."

Chas must have been a real lady's man in his day—he was a natural.

Pretending to be dead felt kind of strange. I'd found a spare room, climbed into bed, and waited. Sooner or later I knew that one of the staff would check the open door. Sure enough, just over an hour later, I heard footsteps come into the room. That was my cue to cast the 'still' spell. It was risky because I'd only had chance to practise it once before. The spell stopped my heart. It was a scary sensation—knowing that my heart was no longer pumping, but the spell somehow kept me alive.

The nurse lifted my hand and checked for a pulse. Then she tried my neck. After a couple of minutes, a doctor joined her. He took only a few moments to confirm her diagnosis. "Time of death, three-forty five pm."

I lay there for another thirty minutes before I was transferred onto a trolley, and wheeled down a series of corridors to what I assumed must be the mortuary.

"I don't have any records for her," a male voice said.

"Nothing?"

"No. There wasn't meant to be anyone in that room. No one seems to know anything about her except Chas."

The other man laughed. "Trust Chas. He never misses an opportunity."

"What do you want me to do?"

"Leave her with me. Someone will claim her sooner or later."

The first man left.

"So who are you, darling?" The man lifted the sheet off my right arm, then walked around the trolley and lifted it off my left arm.

"What have we here?" He took my hand. I rarely wore jewellery, but had put on the ring which Kathy had bought me for my twenty-first birthday. It wasn't particularly expensive, but it might have fetched a few pounds.

"Come on!" He pulled at the ring. "There you go!"

He pocketed it, turned to me and said, "Thank you, darling. Just you wait there, I'll be right back."

He'd no sooner walked out the door than I reversed the 'still' spell, and then reversed the 'ageing' spell. It felt good to get my younger body back, and even better to feel my heart beating again. I was out of the morgue in time to see him disappear through a door at the far end of the corridor.

He spun around when he heard me enter the room. "Who are you? What do you want?"

"All of the jewellery you've stolen from the dead."

"I don't know what you're talking about."

"Well for starters, I'm talking about this ring." I pushed my hand into his pocket, and grabbed my ring.

"Who are you?" His face was full of rage now.

"I'm the person who is going to hand you over to the police."

He almost caught me off guard with the first punch, but I managed to duck just in time. His hand hit the door behind me with a thud. Now he was really angry. I cast the 'power' spell in time to catch the second punch. I twisted his arm up his back, turned him around and pushed him hard, face first into the wall. The crack I heard was probably his nose breaking judging by the stream of blood which ran from it. He crumpled onto the floor. I picked up the large padded envelope, which he'd dropped, and tipped its contents onto the desktop. There was an assortment of rings, bracelets and necklaces. Even though I'd never seen it, I instinctively knew which was my mother's ring. I pocketed it, put the rest back in the envelope, and then made my way to the manager's office. En-route, I walked by Chas who stared at me open-mouthed.

"That anti-ageing cream is really good," I said, and gave him a wink.

The manager was in a meeting with his second in command, but he soon agreed to see me when I threatened to call the police. I threw the padded envelope onto his desk, and told him he had one week to find the owners of the jewellery, otherwise I would get the place closed down. He looked genuinely horrified to learn what had happened, and promised to do what I asked. He also promised that the offender would be off the premises within the hour.

I know. I know. I should have called the police, but how would I have explained my presence there? The main thing was that I had my mother's ring. Plus I'd given Chas a great story to tell—not that anyone would believe him.

I saw it, but I still didn't believe it. How was it possible? The first time had been a shock, but a second time?

Something was seriously wrong with the world order. The woman on Mr Ivers' arm this time was a leggy brunette with a tattoo of a dolphin on her right shoulder. She was much younger than him, and could have graced any catwalk. My curiosity needed to be satisfied.

"Mr Ivers!" I stepped out from behind a tree. "How are you?"

"We're just on our way out." He tried to sidestep me, but I was too quick.

"We?" I had to know who the mystery woman was.

"This is Dee." He beamed at his companion.

"DeeDee actually," she squeaked. "But everyone calls me Dee."

"Dee? Right. Nice to meet you, Dee."

"We have to be going," Ivers said.

"Going to the movies?"

"Movies? No. Why would you think that?"

"I just thought—the newsletter—?"

"I've given that up. We're going for a Chinese. Got to rush." He didn't risk the sidestep this time. Instead, he gently shoulder charged me aside.

What was going on? The man had gone from film nerd to Casanova, seemingly overnight. How could that have happened? And more importantly, how was it that Mr Ivers could pull, and I couldn't?

# Chapter 12

"He pretty much kept himself to himself," Terry Woodyer said.

"Yeah. We tried to include him in things, but he always found some excuse," Dawn Treadmore agreed.

Terry and Dawn worked in the same office as Norman Reeves. They'd been reluctant to talk to me at first because they thought I was hell-bent on blaming Norman for the disappearance of the holiday cash. Only when I'd managed to convince them that I had an open mind, did they relent.

"You both got on okay with him then?"

"He was very shy. People who didn't know him thought he was strange, but really he was just very awkward," Dawn said.

"What did you think when you heard about the holiday money going missing?" I asked.

"That it couldn't have been Norman," Terry said. Dawn nodded in agreement.

"You seem very sure."

"I don't believe Norman would ever steal anything. He didn't seem to care about money," Dawn said. "He was one of the most honest, generous people I've ever met."

"If he didn't take the money, why do you think he disappeared?"

"I don't know." Dawn frowned. "I'm really worried about him."

"Had he been acting strangely at all before he went missing?

"Not really. No more than usual, anyway."

"*Anything* you can remember might help."

"It's just that—" Dawn hesitated. "When he started seeing Natasha, I was like—wow!—Norman has a girlfriend?"

Terry nodded. "He was shy and awkward at the best of times, but around girls, he was a nervous wreck."

"It took him months before he could make eye contact with me." Dawn smiled.

"How did he and Natasha meet?"

"As far as we could make out, he got talking to her in a coffee shop," Terry said.

"It must have been the other way around." Dawn corrected him. "There's no way Norman would have made the first move."

"Did he talk about Natasha much?" I asked.

"Not really. Not unless we asked, and even then he never went into detail. He hadn't seen her for a few days, so I was beginning to think that maybe it was over. I didn't like to ask."

Winky was sulking underneath my desk.
"What's wrong with you?" I said.
He shrugged.
"Is it because I won't let you use the computer?"
"Nah, I can get on there any time I like."
He probably could.
"What's wrong then?"
"She's gone."
"You're going to have to give me more than that."
"Bella."
"Your semaphore buddy?"
"Yeah. I haven't seen her since yesterday."
"Maybe she's out catching mice or something."

"Bella does *not* catch mice."

"Don't all cats catch mice?"

"That's a cover for the benefit of humans."

"To hide the fact that you're really hacking computers?"

"Bella isn't a hacker. She's an actress and model."

"Catwalk?"

"You're hilarious. Have you seen the latest CatDreams ad?"

"Can't say I have."

"Check it out. She looks divine in that."

"Maybe she's out on a shoot."

"No. She definitely said she'd be in her window last night, but nothing. Same again today. You have to do something."

"What am I supposed to do?"

"You're a private investigator aren't you? Go investigate stuff."

I eventually managed to placate Winky with the promise that I'd investigate Bella's disappearance as soon as I'd finished up at the office. The computer screen prompted me for my password, but when I entered it, it spat it back out. I tried again with the same result.

"I've changed it to 'ILoveBella'," Winky shouted from under the desk.

As soon as I signed into the dating website, a small red flag began to blink in the top right-hand corner of the screen. I had three messages.

The first was a generic welcome message from the site's admin. The other two were from members who had responded to my profile. Daze had given me the name of the Rogue she was trying to ensnare, and sure enough he was one of the two respondents. She had obviously done her homework in creating a profile which would attract his attention.

I gave Daze a call.

"Jill? Hold on a minute, would you?"

"I can call back later—"

She'd obviously moved the phone away from her ear. I could hear her voice and another—a man's—on the other end of the line.

"You can't give me a ticket!"

"You're illegally parked, sir."

"Technically speaking, maybe. But I always nip in here for a coffee. I've only been gone a minute."

"One minute too long."

"Can't we come to some arrangement?"

"Are you trying to bribe me, sir?"

"No. Not at all. I'm just saying—"

"There you go sir, have a nice day." "Jill? Sorry about that."

"Sounds like you're beginning to enjoy the new job."

"It has its moments."

"I've had a reply from Damon Black."

"Great. I thought he'd *bite*." She chuckled at her own joke. "Have you replied to him yet?"

"No. I was waiting until I'd checked in with you. When do you want to do this?"

"The sooner that scum-bag is behind bars in Candlefield, the better."

I'd no sooner posted my reply to Damon Black, than my phone rang. It was Jack Maxwell.

"Hi, Jack. Do you need someone to whup you at bowling again?"

"Funny, very funny. Look, I wouldn't normally do this, but I know your sister was one of the people affected by the holiday fund theft."

"What's happened?"

"Norman Reeves' car has been found."

"What about him?"

"No. Still no sign."

"And the money?"

"Just the car, so far."

"Where was it?"

"Parked on the ground floor of the long-stay car park next to the train station. Looks like our friend, Norman might have done a runner."

"I'm not buying that."

"Why? What do you know that I don't?"

"Nothing really, but I've spoken to some of his work colleagues. According to them, he's as honest as the day is long."

"They all are—until they're not."

I knew Maxwell was right. People could change. How well did anyone really know the people they worked with? "Okay. Well thanks for letting me know."

"Don't forget. This arrangement has to work both ways—if you know anything—you tell me. Understood?"

"Absolutely. Could I take a look at the car?"

"There's nothing much to see, but sure knock yourself out. I'll let the officer down there know you're coming."

"Don't forget about Bella!" Winky called after me, as I left the office.

"Don't worry, I'm on it."

This new working relationship with Maxwell was kind

of unnerving. When we'd hated each other's guts, I'd known precisely where I stood. Now, I didn't know how to play it. Maybe I should have reported the Daleside affair, but how would I have explained being on the scene wearing 'old lady' clothes? From now on, I'd do my best to play ball. Maybe.

It wasn't difficult to spot Reeves' car. It was cordoned off by bright yellow tape with the words 'Police - do not cross' printed on it. The solitary policeman standing guard must have drawn the short straw. He eyed me suspiciously.

"Jill Gooder." I flashed him my *sweetest* smile.

He remained stony faced. I had a way with men.

"Detective Maxwell said it would be okay for me to take a look at the car."

He still said nothing—obviously the strong, silent type.

"Hello?"

"Go ahead."

I was getting a certain vibe. Something told me he'd read the Bugle article, and wasn't a fan.

"Thanks." I ducked under the tape. Norman Reeves was obviously the kind of guy who took good care of his car. It was ten years old, but looked as though it had just come out of the showroom. I checked the door pockets and the glove compartment—nothing. I pushed back the seats to check if there was anything underneath—nothing. After thirty minutes, I'd seen all there was to see, which was precisely nothing.

"Anything on CCTV?" I asked Mr Happy.

"Nothing. Camera's out." He gestured towards the camera mounted on the wall, above the emergency exit.

I took a closer look. Sure enough, it looked as though

someone had taken a hammer to it.

It took me a few minutes to locate the security office. The man had his feet up on the desk, and was playing a game on his phone.

"Hi." I stuck my head around the door.

He grunted.

"I'm working with the police—with Detective Maxwell."

He grunted again, still more interested in the game.

"What happened to the camera on the ground floor? The one near the entrance."

He shrugged. "They're always getting smashed up."

"When did it happen?"

"Last week some time."

Mrs V wasn't happy.

"I'm not happy." She sighed.

See, what did I tell you?

"What's the matter?" I took a sneaky glance at her legs—just in case.

"I don't know. It's never happened to me before."

I waited for more.

"I've been doing this for the best part of sixty years."

And waited.

"Why should it start now?"

Any time now.

"I keep dropping stitches."

There we go—worth the wait, no?

"I wouldn't worry about it. I had the same problem."

She fixed me with her gaze.

"What?"

"You aren't seriously trying to draw a comparison

between me, a regional competition winner, and you? Are you?"

"No. Of course not. I only meant it can happen to anyone."

"Not to me. Annabel Versailles did not become a regional champion by dropping stitches."

"I suppose not."

"Something is amiss."

"How do you mean?"

"Sabotage." She looked furtively around the room. I followed her gaze.

"Sabotage?"

"There are a lot of people who would like to see me lose my crown. They must have interfered with my needles."

"How would they do that?"

"I don't know, but nowadays everything is digital isn't it? Anything is possible."

I could feel a migraine coming on.

"Maybe we should get the office swept," she said.

"The cleaner comes in every other night."

"Not that kind of swept. Swept for devices."

"What kind of devices?"

"Knitting needle jammers or blockers or whatever it is that they're using."

Sure. I'll give them a call. What's the number again? Oh yes, Crazytown911. "Okay. I'll see what I can do."

"Thank you!" Winky began to rub up against my leg. "You're the best!"

Now, I was scared. "What's wrong with you?"

"Thank you for finding Bella."

"Bella?" I'd forgotten all about the missing feline

supermodel.

"She's back. I thought I'd lost her."

"Did she say anything? With her flags, I mean?"

"She must have lost them."

"So you haven't actually been able to exchange messages, then?"

"No. Just loving glances."

In that case, I totally found her. "It was nothing. Pleased I could help."

"I owe you. If there's anything you need."

"I don't suppose you know anything about digital knitting needle jammers, do you?"

To escape the madness I took a walk down the high street. The coffee was more expensive than in my office, but there was less of the crazy. I sat at a window seat, and did a quick mental review of the cases I was working on. I'd recovered my mother's ring, so that was one down. I hadn't made much headway with the missing holiday funds. As for the one paying case on my books, I was still waiting to hear back from Seamus-the-wheel. I was due to give Colonel Briggs an update, and we'd arranged to meet at the dog show in a few days time. He thought it might be helpful for me to talk to some of the people who had known Mrs Vicars from the Dog Show circuit.

The coffee shop was on the opposite side of the road to Ever a Wool Moment. From my seat, I could see a steady stream of customers going into the shop. Grandma might be many things—most of them unprintable—but she knew the yarn market.

That's when it struck me. Grandma wasn't one to give in easily, but she definitely was one to hold a grudge. She must have hated having to back down over Mrs V's toad legs. How better to take her revenge than to put some kind of curse on Mrs V's knitting? No wonder she was losing stitches, and it had nothing to do with digital knitting needle jammers.

Time for another showdown.

As I waited for the lights to change, I spotted a familiar face coming towards me. Natasha Cutts' face looked like thunder, and she became quite animated, as she screamed into the phone.

"Natasha?"

It took her a moment to register who I was. "Oh, hi." She pressed the 'end call' button.

"Sorry, I didn't mean to interrupt."

"That's okay. It was just—err—my mother."

"Are you okay? You seemed kind of upset."

She smiled nervously. "I'm fine. You know what mothers are like."

I nodded. She should try having a ghost-witch for a mother.

"I'd better get going," she said, and was gone.

"Don't you have any work to do?" Grandma said when I walked into her shop.

"Reverse the spell," I said.

"I already did. Her legs are perfectly normal now."

"That's not what I meant, and you know it."

"I don't know what you're talking about."

"What I said before still stands. I'll never go to Candlefield again, and I'll—"

"Renounce your witchmanship, blah, blah, blah."

"I mean it, Mrs V is off limits. Reverse the spell which is

making her drop stiches."

"You're no fun at all, are you?" Grandma sighed. "Okay, I've reversed it."

"No more, okay?"

"Okay, I get the message. Mrs V is off limits. Happy now?"

For now maybe, but something told me I was going to be made to suffer for this later.

# Chapter 13

"Mum?" It still felt kind of weird doing this. "Mum?"

"Yes, dear?" My mother's ghost appeared behind me. "Is everything okay?" She was standing/hovering just in front of the French doors.

"Everything's fine. How are the wedding preparations going?"

"Getting there. How's your speech coming along?"

Speech? What speech? "Err—nicely."

"Is there something you need? I was in the middle of making breakfast for Alberto. He loves a good fry up."

"I have something for you." I took the ring out of my pocket, and held it out to her. Her hand began to tremble.

"Mum? Are you okay?"

She put a hand to her mouth; tears were welling in her eyes.

"Mum?"

"I'm okay," she managed. "Just give me a moment." She reached out and took the ring. "How? How did you know?"

"Alberto told me. Don't be mad at him."

The initial shock over, she moved over to the sofa. "Come here." She patted the seat beside her. "I'm not mad at him. How could I be?"

"You should have told me about the ring," I said.

"I didn't want to bother you. I knew you'd feel obliged to do something about it, and you already had enough on your plate."

"It's beautiful." I touched the ring as it lay on her open palm.

"It'll be yours one day."

I smiled, unsure exactly how that would work, but for once in my life, too diplomatic to ask.

"My wedding day will be complete now," she said. "I have everything I need. The man that I love, my grandmother's ring, and my beautiful daughter."

Both of us were in tears now.

"You'd better get back to Alberto's fry up," I said, wiping my eyes.

"Thank you again." She was still staring at the ring when she disappeared.

Speech? No one had said anything to me about a speech. What was I meant to say exactly? I'd only known my mother for a matter of weeks, and then only as a ghost. Should the speech be serious? Funny? I knew nothing of the conventions of sup or ghost marriages, and I highly doubted I'd find a book on it in the local library. I was going to need help. Aunt Lucy's help.

I called Kathy to let her know that Norman Reeves' car had been found.

"What does that mean?" she asked.

"The police think he abandoned it there, and left on a train."

"What do you think?"

"The evidence certainly points that way."

"That's not what I asked, Jill. What do *you* think?"

"The more I learn about him, the less likely it seems that he'd steal the cash. If his co-workers are to be believed, he's a shy, honest man who would be horrified at having an overdue library book. The problem is he isn't here to defend himself. Maybe he did do it. Stranger things have happened."

"So is that it? Do we kiss goodbye to the money?"

"I still have a few leads to follow up, but I wouldn't want to get your hopes up."

"What about Candlefield? Have you managed to sort anything out yet?"

"I'll be seeing Aunt Lucy later today. I'll keep you posted."

As I made my way out of the flat, I heard what sounded like someone crying.

"Hello?" I said.

The young woman stepped out from the alcove where the mail-boxes were located. Her eyes were red and puffy, and her make-up had run, so it took a few seconds for me to realise it was DeeDee aka Dee.

"Are you okay?" I asked.

"Yes." She sobbed. "I'm being silly."

"What's happened?"

She broke down in tears again. I hated it when people cried; I was never sure what to do. "There, there." I put a hand on her shoulder. I'd seen Kathy do that with Lizzie.

I waited until she'd cried herself out. "Okay now?"

She nodded. "He's a pig."

"Mr Ivers?"

"Ivy, yeah. He's a pig."

"What happened?"

"He dumped me."

"*He* dumped *you*?"

She sobbed again. "Yeah."

"Did he say why?"

"He's found someone else."

That would make number three, in the space of a week.

"How did you meet Mr—Ivy?"

"At the Regent."

"The hotel near the station?"

She nodded. "They have a speed dating night there once a week."

"You met Mr Ivers at a speed dating night?"

"Yeah. We hit it off straight away."

"If you don't mind me asking, what kind of thing did he talk about? The movies?"

"Movies? No. I don't actually remember what we talked about. He was just so—" She hesitated. "Fascinating and funny. I'd never met anyone like him. And now, he's dumped me."

She broke down in tears again.

It was another ten minutes before she'd regained composure enough to go on her way. What was I missing? The man was a certified bore, and was no looker. How had he landed himself not one, not two, but three dates? Why was a beautiful young woman like Dee in floods of tears because he'd dumped her? It made zero sense. My 'something's fishy' meter was sounding. I'd already signed up for an online dating site; why not give speed dating a try too?

I gave Aunt Lucy a call to ask if I could go over to see her later that day. I wanted to pick her brains about the wedding speech I was supposed to deliver, and to see if she had any bright ideas on how I should handle the 'Kathy/Candlefield' situation.

Mrs V looked much happier; her knitting needles were

moving at warp speed.

"Everything okay?" I asked.

"Lovely."

"No more dropped stitches?"

"Not a single one. How did you manage to sort it out?"

"I had them install an anti-jamming device. You shouldn't have any more problems."

"Thank you, dear. I knew I could rely on you."

What? What was I supposed to tell her?

"This came for you." She handed me an envelope.

Seamus-the-wheel had prepared a short report: Hector Vicars had a five year ban for drink driving, effectively ending what had been a promising amateur career in rally driving. So much for 'retiring at the top'. He didn't currently have a car registered in his name.

Hilary Vicars had a dark blue Saab registered in her name. It had never been reported to the police as stolen, but Seamus had managed to track it to a breaker's yard. He'd located it before the vehicle had been crushed, and he'd paid the yard owner to hold onto it until Seamus gave him the nod.

In the spirit of our new style co-operation, I updated Maxwell on my findings in the Vicars case. I told him about Hilary's car, and what Mrs Draycott had told me about Edna Vicars' final words. He said he'd get someone to check out the car, but he was sceptical about what Mrs Draycott had supposedly heard.

"Calling for her son when she knew she was dying? That's hardly surprising."

"You don't think she might have been trying to tell Mrs

Draycott who was responsible for her death? Who was behind the wheel?"

"It's possible, but I'm going to need a lot more proof before I can arrest him."

"How's the love life?" I asked Winky who was perched in his usual spot on the window sill.

"Don't ask."

"Has Bella gone AWOL again?"

"No. She's there. Look!"

Sure enough, beautiful Bella, the feline supermodel, was in her usual spot across the way.

"Who is she signalling to?"

"You might well ask." Winky sighed.

Winky's flags were by his side on the window sill.

"Is she two-timing you?"

"If I find out who he is, I'll cut his nuts off." Winky hissed.

"Have you asked her why?"

"She says she doesn't want to get serious."

"Supermodels. They can be like that." Obviously, I spoke as a leading authority on the subject. "How about some dinner?"

"I'm not hungry."

Crazy, psycho Winky was exhausting, but sad Winky was kind of heartbreaking.

It didn't take long to find out that Natasha Cutts worked as a temp with the QuickTemp Agency which was located a few streets from my office.

"Good morning," the young woman said. The name on her badge was Peach. Poor girl.

"Morning, I'd like to sign up as a temp."

"Sure. Follow me." Peach led me behind a blue screen, and gestured for me to take a seat.

"I'll need to take a few details from you."

"Fire away."

"Name?"

"Jasmine Pear." What? If she can be a peach, I can be a pear.

"Address?"

"10 Apple Drive, Washbridge." Too much? I have to keep myself amused somehow—it helps me get through the day.

Peach gave me a look. I smiled reassuringly.

"What type of position are you looking for?"

I can't tell you how tempted I was to say 'fruit picker', but I decided that might be a step too far.

"Receptionist."

"What experience do you have?"

"I've been working in a solicitor's office for the last four years."

"That's good. What's the name of the firm?"

"Cherry, Cherry and Berry." I just couldn't help myself.

"I've never heard of them."

I'd had my fun. Now it was time to get to work.

The sound was almost deafening. Papers lifted off desks and began to swirl around the room in a vortex of air. Peach was pushed back in her chair by the sheer force of the wind.

"What's happening?" I said. If only Washbridge Amdram could see me now, they'd sign me up on the spot.

"I don't know." Peach struggled off her chair, and

began to fight her way to the front of the room. The other staff were desperately trying to gather papers and files that had been scattered all over the floor.

For my first attempt at the 'vortex' spell, that had gone very well. Not only had I judged the power just right, but I'd also positioned it so that I escaped the worst of the devastation.

"What's happening?" a male voice said.

"I don't know," Peach sounded almost hysterical. "It's like a whirlwind or something."

I grabbed the mouse, clicked on the menu option, and selected 'name search'. Fortunately there was only one Natasha Cutts listed. I had a notepad to jot down the names of the companies she'd worked for, but when I saw the third one on the list, I knew I had what I needed.

The mini tornado had run its course. I switched back to the screen where Peach had been entering my details.

"Sorry," Peach said. "I really don't know what just happened."

"Not to worry. I can see you're busy. I'll come back some other time."

"Sorry again."

"You might want to get your air conditioning looked at," I said, on my way out.

The power station had been a victim of the transition away from fossil fuels. Despite a petition, signed by over twenty thousand people worried about local jobs, the plant had closed. Decommissioning and demolition were scheduled for the following year, according to press reports. In the meantime, the buildings stood as a bleak reminder of lost jobs and livelihoods. The perimeter was protected by a tall, steel fence topped with razor wire. Signs warned would-be intruders that the site was protected by guard dogs.

My previous attempt at levitation had been something of a disaster, and a source of much amusement to Grandma. This fence was much taller, and the razor wire would be a lot less forgiving. I couldn't afford to make a mistake.

I rose gradually off the ground until I was a foot above the razor wire, and then edged slowly forward until I was clear of the fence. Now came the difficult part. This was where I'd got it spectacularly wrong last time when instead of a slow, controlled descent, I'd dropped like a stone. I was wiser and more experienced now, and determined not to give Grandma any more ammunition to use against me. She'd already be gunning for me after the Mrs V incident.

Slowly does it. Perfect! I was on the ground, and not a bruise or cut to be seen. Now, all I had to worry about was the three dogs which were racing towards me—teeth bared.

# Chapter 14

They looked so very peaceful now. The 'sleep' spell had done its job, but it had been a close call. I'd had to wait until the dogs were close enough, before casting the spell on each of them in turn. The last of the three had almost been on me when he slumped to the ground.

The site was divided into two distinct areas: the power station itself with its huge cooling towers to my right, and to my left, the expansive office buildings. Nature was already beginning to reclaim the land, with weeds growing out of every crack in the concrete.

The large double doors were locked, but I soon found a broken window—there were plenty of them. Inside it was cold and damp. Everything of any value had long since been stripped out. It would have taken me all day to search every office, but I had a better idea. The 'listen' spell brought the building to life. A million and one sounds invaded my head. Water dripping—maybe a broken pipe or a tap. A thousand small feet—the place was no doubt home to any number of rats, mice and creepy crawlies. And then, from somewhere among that cacophony came what sounded like a voice. A very weak voice. I re-focussed, this time filtering out all other sounds.

I headed towards the voice, being careful not to stumble over the debris which was scattered everywhere. When I reached the stairs, I hesitated. The voice had fallen silent. After a few seconds, it started up again—barely audible even with the 'listen' spell. I reached the top floor, and followed the voice along the corridor—hugging the wall. The sign on the door read 'Conference room 3A'. The small glass window in the door was broken. Through it I could see him.

The man tied to the chair was tall and gangly. The only light in the room came from a broken skylight above his head. I pushed the door open slowly. I was conscious there might be others in the room. Once inside, I began to walk slowly towards the man. His head was bowed, so he didn't see my approach until I was only a few feet away.

"Help me!" His voice was weak. "Please, help me."

After untying him, I made a call to Maxwell.

"I've found Norman Reeves. He's going to need an ambulance."

Thirty minutes later, Norman Reeves was in A&E, and I was in my favourite interview room with my favourite detective.

"You should have called us before you went charging in there."

"I wasn't sure he'd be there. It was just a hunch."

"Some hunch. How did you know?"

"I think Reeves was actually abducted before the night that he and Natasha supposedly visited the restaurant. Reeves is a skinny giant. The man on the restaurant CCTV was only a few inches taller than Natasha—I'd hazard a guess that was Dominic Whitelaw. Also, the driver's seat in the abandoned car was pushed all the way forward. There's no way Reeves could have driven with the seat in that position. Natasha or Dominic must have driven it to the car park—they probably took out the only CCTV camera the day before. They needed to make it look like Reeves had taken a train."

"How did you put Cutts and Whitelaw together?"

"Natasha Cutts works for a temp agency. Three years ago she was assigned to work at the power station. Her boss was Dominic Whitelaw. I'm pretty sure they've been having an affair ever since."

"That still doesn't explain how you knew where to find Reeves."

"Whitelaw still has access to the power plant. He's been overseeing its closure. Like I said, it was just a hunch. Reeves should be able to fill in the blanks when he's recovered."

"He was lucky you found him when you did. I've spoken to the doctor at A&E. She said another twenty four hours and he probably wouldn't have made it. The only reason he's still alive now is because he managed to catch a few drops of rainwater which had dripped in through the broken skylight."

"What's going to happen to them now?"

"Natasha Cutts and Dominic Whitelaw are being taken into custody as we speak."

"And the money?"

"That's anyone's guess."

"Will you let me know if it turns up? I want to tell Kathy. Hopefully, it'll be good news."

I stood up.

"Whoa, just a minute. We aren't done yet."

I sat back down.

"You haven't explained how you managed to view the CCTV from the restaurant or how you managed to gain access to the power station."

"A lady has to have some secrets."

I decided to drive to Candlefield. It was much slower

than casting a spell, but it was way more relaxing.

"Jill!" Aunt Lucy greeted me with a hug. "Come on in. I was about to make a cup of tea. Would you like one?"

"That would be great."

"Milk. One and two-thirds spoonfuls of sugar?"

"Please."

"Your mother tells me that you found her ring. She was so thrilled."

"I was thrilled for her. She did say something that confused me though."

"Oh? What's that?"

"She said the ring would pass down to me."

"And so it will."

"Yeah, but that's the bit I don't understand. Normally possessions are passed down when someone dies, but my mother—well—"

"I see what you mean. It's simple really. Your mother will only be a ghost for as long as she chooses to be. After that her spirit will move on."

"Move on?"

"That's right. In fact, the only reason she chose to remain here as a ghost was because she wanted to make sure that you were safe. She didn't know how you'd cope with the transition to being a witch." Aunt Lucy took a sip of tea. "She needn't have worried on that score."

"So she could leave at any time?"

"In theory, yes. But then again it could be decades or even centuries from now."

"I'll be long gone by then anyway." I laughed.

"Not necessarily."

"What do you mean?"

"You haven't realised, have you? As a witch, you don't

age in the same way as a human does."

"No one told me that."

"I'm sorry dear. There's so much we take for granted. I forget sometimes that this is all still new to you. Witches are not immortal, but they do age much slower than humans—probably one tenth as fast."

Maths was never my strong point, but I did the calculation.

"So a witch could be six hundred years old, but only appear to be sixty?"

"Thereabouts. It's way more complicated than that. The more time you spend in the human world, the quicker you will age."

"Do all witches live to such a great age?"

"Not all. Just like humans, some fall victim to illness or injury. Like I said, witches are not immortal. Although your body will withstand much more than that of a human, and will recover much quicker, you're not invincible."

"How old is Grandma?"

"In human years? About eight hundred and fifty."

"No wonder she's cranky."

Aunt Lucy laughed.

"I'm afraid I've had a couple of run-ins with her recently," I said. "Since she opened the wool shop."

"Don't worry your head about it. I'd be more surprised if you hadn't. She'd try the patience of a saint. How is her shop doing?"

"Very well as far as I can tell. She's a mean marketeer, I'll give her that."

Aunt Lucy made us a snack, and said, "You mentioned

you wanted to talk to me about the wedding."

"Mum said I'll be expected to give a speech. That's the first I've heard of it."

"Just keep it simple. Say a few words about what it means to be reunited with your mother. That will have everyone in tears—except Grandma of course. Then wish the happy couple well, and you're done."

"Aren't there any special witch formalities or customs I need to be aware of?"

"No. The ceremony is pretty much what you'd expect in the human world. Incidentally, have the girls mentioned the hen night to you?"

"No." I hated hen nights with a passion.

"They will. They've been talking about nothing else."

"It's not really my kind of thing."

"They're going to be disappointed if you don't go."

Great.

"The main reason I wanted to see you," I said, trying hard to put the hen night out of my mind, "was about Kathy, and her family."

"Are they okay?"

"Yeah, they're fine. It's just that when I came to my mother's funeral, I didn't know the rules about not telling humans about Candlefield. Anyway, I told Kathy, and now she wants to come over with the family. I don't know what to do."

"You've tried the 'forget' spell I take it?"

"Yeah, but it doesn't seem to unseat the memory from when I originally told her. Peter and the kids know too. The holiday they'd planned has fallen through, so now Kathy has had the brilliant idea of them all coming here. I'm supposed to ask you if they can stay with you."

"Oh dear. That is a bit of a mess."

"No kidding."

"Leave it with me, and I'll see what I can come up with."

# Chapter 15

"Please, pretty please," Amber said.

"You have to come, Jill." Pearl could have won medals for pouting.

"Hen nights really aren't my thing. I'm getting too old for that kind of thing."

"Nonsense. You're not much older than us. Please say you'll come."

It was my own fault. I should have steered clear of Cuppy C. Aunt Lucy had warned me that they were hell-bent on getting me to go on the hen night.

"How many people are going?" I asked.

"Including you?"

"Excluding me."

"Two."

"Two others apart from you two?"

Pearl frowned. "No, just us two."

"What about my mother? She's the one getting married."

"A lot of the clubs are a bit sniffy about letting ghosts in. And, besides she told Mum that she was too old for that kind of thing. She wants you to go though."

I studied Amber's face. Had my mother really said that or was it just a ploy to get me to agree? "What about Aunt Lucy?"

The twins shared the same horrified expression. "Mum?" Pearl said. "We don't want her there."

"She doesn't want to come anyway," Amber said. "She can't bear to be separated from Lester. Yuk!"

"I like Lester." Although I still hadn't got used to his moustache.

"*You* don't have to watch them smooching. It shouldn't be allowed."

"So, then." I finished off the last few crumbs of the strawberry cupcake. "The hen night is just you two?"

"And you," Pearl said.

"Please!" Amber pleaded.

Saying no would have felt like smacking a kitten. "Go on then. But I'm not staying out too late. I've got a lot on at the moment."

"Yay!"

"Thank you!"

They hugged me.

"Now we have to decide what you're going to wear." Amber was the first to release me.

"You need something new and spectacular!" Pearl said.

Spectacular?

"We have to go shopping right now!" Pearl began to take off her apron.

"What about the shop?"

"Amber can look after it."

"No way!" Amber threw her apron onto the table. "If you're going, so am I."

"It's your turn to hold the fort." Pearl had her arms crossed — she meant business.

"What about yesterday when you went out to get your nails done?"

"That was an emergency."

"You'd only had them done the day before."

"One of them was chipped."

"I'm sure I can manage to go shopping alone if you two are needed here."

They turned their gaze on me, and then back to one

another—and laughed.

"What?"

"You're so funny, Jill," Amber said.

What? I was capable of picking out clothes.

"You may be kicking our asses with level two spells, but—" Pearl looked me up and down. "Seriously?"

"I look okay, don't I?" I was wearing my favourite grey slacks and a freshly ironed white blouse.

"You look *okay*, but you have to look *spectacular!*" Pearl said.

"I do?"

"Definitely," they said in unison. Well at least I'd got them to agree on something—my fashion sense sucked.

Neither of the twins had any intention of missing out on a morning's shopping, so they left Cuppy C in the hands of their two assistants, who if I read their body language correctly, weren't particularly sorry to see their employers leave.

Before we set off for the shops, the twins decided that it would be a good idea for me to see the outfits that each of them had bought for the hen night. They said it would give me an idea of what 'spectacular' looked like. Neither girl had seen the other's outfit yet.

I stood in the corridor, outside the twins' bedrooms.

"Ready?" Amber called.

"Ready!" Pearl replied.

I took a deep breath. I had a horrible feeling that I wasn't going to like 'spectacular', but I couldn't let my feelings show. Whatever the girls were wearing, I'd say I loved it. I just wished I was a better liar.

"Three, two—" Amber began the countdown. "One!"

The two bedroom doors flew open, and out stepped

'spectacular'.

Amber was closest to me, and she saw the look on my face.

"What? Don't you like it?"

"You did it on purpose!" Pearl screamed.

Amber spun around to face her sister.

"I bought mine first! You can take yours back!"

If I'd laughed, they'd have probably killed me. The blue mini dress that Amber was wearing was indeed spectacular. So was the identical one worn by Pearl.

"How was I supposed to know you'd bought that?" Pearl screamed. "You should have told me."

"I asked if you wanted to see my outfit, but you said 'no'. You said I had no taste!"

"Maybe you could both wear the same?" I said.

The twins turned their gazes on me.

"Or not. Daft idea. Scrub that."

"So what are we going to do?" Pearl said.

"I'm not taking mine back."

"Neither am I."

And so it was decided. All three of us would look for a new outfit.

The duplicate dress incident actually worked in my favour because the twins would now be focused on their own purchases instead of mine. It was remarkable how similar their tastes were. Every time one of them spotted a dress they liked, the other one homed in on it too.

"I saw it first!"

"In your dreams!"

"Girls, girls." I stepped in. "You'll tear it."

"I saw it first, Jill," Amber said.

"She's a liar. I'd already picked it up."

This was worse than a shopping expedition with Kathy's kids. At least they didn't fight over the same toys.

"Enough!" I said, in my school headmistress voice. "This can't go on."

"It's her fault!"

"It's yours."

"Shush, both of you. If you don't stop this, I am not going on the hen night."

"But—"

"Shush."

"It's—"

"Shush!"

I waited until I had silence and their full attention. "Okay, this is how it's going to work." I took out a coin. "Amber, call. Heads or tails?"

They shared the same puzzled expression.

"Heads or tails?"

She called heads. I tossed the coin.

"It's tails. Pearl you get to choose. Right or left?"

"I don't understand—"

"Pick one. Right or left."

She shrugged. "Right."

"Okay. You have to stay on the right-hand side of the high street. Amber you have to stick to the left."

"But Michy's is on the left," Pearl said.

"Firstme is on the right." Amber complained.

"It's swings and roundabouts. There are enough shops here for both of you to find something. Agreed?"

The twins pouted, then shrugged, but finally agreed.

"What about you?" Pearl said. "Which one of us are you going with?"

"Neither of you. I'll choose something for myself."

They both laughed.

"I promise to choose something 'spectacular'. You can both meet me back here in two hours. I promise I won't actually buy anything until you've approved it. How's that?"

They reluctantly agreed and hurried off.

Now, all I had to do was find something spectacular.

The moment I spotted it, I knew I'd found the one. But was I brave enough to try it on, let alone go out in it? I expected the young witch on the fitting room to give me a 'really?' look, but she just handed me a tag.

Kathy had always insisted that I had nicer legs than her, and that I should show them off, but I rarely wore anything above the knee. The red dress was at least an inch shorter than I'd normally wear, but that wasn't the truly spectacular part. Cleavage! Who knew?

"You first Pearl!" Amber insisted when the three of us met up later.

Pearl took out a green dress which made the one I'd tried on look like a maxi.

Amber nodded her approval.

"It's lovely," I agreed.

Amber had chosen a yellow dress which flared out below the waist. A little longer than Pearl's, but with a lower neckline.

Pearl loved it. So did I.

"Now it's your turn." Pearl turned to me.

"Have you found something?" Amber said.

"I have. Follow me."

It felt like prom— not that I'd ever been to prom. The twins were waiting for me outside the fitting rooms. I took one last look in the mirror. I didn't care what they thought, I loved it anyway.

My legs felt like jelly as I walked out. They looked me up and down, glanced at one another, and then said in unison, "Spectacular!"

By nine o'clock the three of us were ready to party, and although I say it myself, we looked hot!

"Party time!" Amber said.

"I feel like dancing." Pearl did a sexy shimmy.

"Me too." The voice came from behind us.

"Grandma?" All three of us said.

Grandma was resplendent in black satin. I'd never seen her wear make-up before, but tonight she'd plastered it on.

"Where are we going first?" She began to shuffle her feet in what was either a dance or the prelude to a seizure.

All colour had drained from Amber and Pearl's faces. "Grandma?"

"Why do you keep saying that?" Grandma began to shake her booty. Something no one should have to witness.

"Are you planning on coming with us?" There was desperation in Pearl's voice.

"Of course I am. Didn't think I'd miss a hen night did you?"

"Mum's staying at home," Amber said.

"Pah. Old before her time that daughter of mine."

"It's going to be noisy," Pearl said.

"And hot," Amber added.

"I can't wait." Grandma made for the door. "Come on, what are you waiting for?"

The three of us shared the look of the condemned.

"We have to lose her," Amber said.

For once, the three of us could agree on something.

First stop was DingDing, a small club that catered mainly for witches and wizards. Although there was no actual policy barring other sups, ninety nine per cent of those inside were witches or wizards. And tonight at least, the ratio was two wizards for every witch.

"How are we meant to pull with her here?" Pearl said when Grandma took a toilet break.

"No one is going to dance with us while she's here." Amber sighed.

"What was that dance she was doing?" We all laughed while keeping an eye open in case she returned.

"You two shouldn't be trying to *pull* anyway," I said. "What about Alan and William?"

"We'll only be flirting. You have to flirt on a hen night — it's the law."

"I hope Grandma doesn't start flirting." I spotted her walking back towards us. "Shhh! She's here."

"This place is lame," Grandma declared. "Let's go somewhere else."

I was already shattered, and ready for bed. "Why don't we find somewhere quiet where we can sit down for a while?"

The twins gave me a look, but it was nothing compared to the one that Grandma shot my way. "Sit down? What's wrong with you? This is meant to be a hen night. You don't 'sit down' on a hen night; you get out on the floor and shake your booty." She gave me a quick demonstration. "All that time you've spent with humans has made you soft. Come on, let's find some real action."

"What are we going to do?" Amber said, in a whisper as the three of us trailed behind Grandma who was shaking her booty all over the street.

"We have to lose her," Pearl said. "This is a disaster."

"If we do, she'll kill us." I kept my eyes on Grandma just in case she turned around.

"Whatever she does to us, it can't be any worse than this," Amber said. "We'll never be able to show our faces again after tonight."

It was now or never. "Quick!" I grabbed the twins and pulled them into the doorway to our right.

"What are you doing?" Pearl said.

"Just follow me."

The maître d' smiled. "Table for three?"

"Yes please. Can we sit over there?" I pointed to the far side of the restaurant.

"I'm not hungry," Amber said, as he led us to our table.

"Just go with it." I picked up a menu and pretended to study it.

"Jill? What are we—?"

"Follow me." I led the way into the kitchen.

"Where's the back exit?" I asked a surprised sous chef. He nodded to his left.

"Run!"

The three of us legged it through the kitchen, out of the door and into an alleyway. Back on the street, I hailed a cab and told him to take us to the other side of Candlefield.

"Anywhere in particular?"

"As far away from here as possible."

# Chapter 16

"We're so dead!" Amber laughed. The cocktail in her hand was a colour I'd never seen in nature.

"She might use magic to track us down." Pearl hadn't taken her gaze from the door since we'd walked into Red, a club that catered for all sups. It was much larger than DingDing, and every bit as noisy.

"Hopefully, she's too drunk to notice." I must have been crazy. I was already in Grandma's bad books because of our run-in over Mrs V. If she knew I'd been the one to instigate the escape plan, I was in serious trouble. "We'd better enjoy tonight, for tomorrow we die. Whose round is it?"

As the night wore on, we began to relax. Maybe Grandma had pulled or was flat out somewhere. We laughed and drank. We danced and drank. We flirted — even I got my fair share of attention. 'Spectacular' had worked — who knew?

The next morning came around much too soon.

"I want to die." Amber was holding her head in her hands.

"I think I already did." Pearl was resting her head on the table.

None of us could face breakfast. It was almost midday, and the three of us had only just made it out of bed.

"What was in that cocktail anyway?" I downed two headache tablets.

"Which one?"

"The orange one."

"I don't know. Nice though weren't they?"

"Nice, but deadly."

"You seemed to be getting rather hot and bothered with that wizard," Amber said to her sister.

"He asked for my number."

"Did you give it to him?"

"I gave him 'a' number. I made one up."

"Who's looking after the shop?" I said.

They both shrugged.

"Don't you think you should check? It might not even be open."

"Amber, you check." Pearl picked up the box of aspirin.

"Why me? You do it."

I couldn't handle the squabbling. "I'll take a look."

Every step I took reverberated inside my head. Never again. I was way too old for this kind of thing. Still, if *I* was feeling bad, how must Grandma be feeling? Maybe she'd been so drunk she'd have forgotten that we ditched her.

"Good morning, Jill."

Either I was still asleep, and this was an alcohol induced nightmare or Grandma was behind the counter.

"Grandma?"

"You look like death warmed up, young lady."

"Why are you here?"

"I figured the twins would be in no fit state to open the shop this morning, so someone had to give these poor girls a hand." She nodded to the two assistants behind the counter who looked duly intimidated. "Jill, why don't you go and get the twins. I'll make us all a nice cup of coffee."

We were so dead!

"Amber, Pearl!"

"Don't shout!" Pearl rubbed her temple.

"Grandma's here."

Suddenly they were awake.

"Here?"

I nodded.

"In the shop?"

I nodded again.

"What's she doing?"

"She's behind the counter."

"How does she look?"

"Better than us, that's for sure."

"What did she say? Did she ask where we disappeared to last night?"

"No. She said she was going to make us coffee, and that I should come and get you."

"We're dead," Amber said.

"So dead. It was all your idea." Pearl pointed at me.

"Hey, don't blame me. You both said you wanted to ditch her."

"We're so dead."

"Take a seat, girls. I'll bring your coffee over." Grandma smiled. That was even more unnerving.

"What's she up to?" Amber whispered.

"Maybe she got so drunk, she's forgotten." Pearl was clutching at straws, and we all knew it.

"There you go!" Grandma arrived with a tray. "You don't mind if I join you do you?"

We all shook our heads.

"It was a great night wasn't it?" Grandma sipped her coffee.

We nodded.

"I had a great time. I must have lost you three somewhere though."

We nodded again.

"Drink your coffee. That will wake you up."

Half an hour later, Grandma had left. The three of us exchanged a look. "What's she up to?" I said.

"Maybe she's forgotten."

"Maybe she got lucky and pulled, so didn't care we weren't there."

"Yeah, that must be it," I said.

"Let me in!" I screamed at the toilet door.

"I haven't finished!" Pearl screamed back.

"I have to go too." Amber was standing beside me now.

"She did this," I said, my buttocks clenched.

"She must have put something in the coffee!"

"Open the door!"

"Open the door, Pearl or I will kill you."

The next three hours were not pretty. One toilet between the three of us — you do the maths.

We were in my bedroom. We had nothing left — literally — it had all been flushed away.

"We should kill her," Amber said.

"Painfully." Pearl squirmed around on the bed, trying to get comfortable.

"How did she survive last night? She's like a million years old, and yet she looks better than we do."

"I'm never going to drink again." Amber hugged a pillow to her chest.

"Or eat." Pearl rubbed her stomach.

"Still," I said. "We did look spectacular."

"Thank you, Jill. Thank you for taking me to the dog show. Is it time to go now? Can we go?" Barry was beside himself with excitement.

"In a minute." I gently pushed him off me. My stomach and head were still very tender.

"Are you sure you're up to this?" Aunt Lucy asked. She and Lester had looked after Barry while the twins and I were on the hen night. Aunt Lucy hadn't mentioned the incident with Grandma, and I thought it best to say nothing.

"Yeah. I promised I'd take him. It might be fun."

Colonel Briggs had given me a ticket to the dog show, which his charity held every year. I'd asked if I could bring Barry along, and he'd said I should enter him into the 'mutts' category which was just a bit of fun.

"Have you prepared your speech for the wedding?" Aunt Lucy said, as she helped to push Barry into the back seat of my car.

"I'm still working on it."

"Good luck at the show."

"Thanks."

I hadn't travelled more than a few miles before Barry had squeezed between the seats, and planted himself in the passenger seat beside me. "I can see better here."

"Stay on your side. Don't get in my way while I'm driving."

"I won't. What's that?"

"It's a post box."

"What's that?"

"It's a bus."

"What's that?"
This was going to be a long journey.

When the colonel had first mentioned the dog show, I'd pictured a low-key event—perhaps in a church hall. I couldn't have been any more wrong. The show took up two large halls at Washbridge's main exhibition centre. I needed all of my strength to hold onto Barry when he heard the sound of a million dogs barking inside.

"This must be Barry." Colonel Briggs had arranged to meet me at the booking-in desk.

Before I could stop him, Barry had launched himself at the colonel.

"Hello, boy. You're a stunner aren't you? Did you enter him for the 'mutt' competition?"

I nodded, but was already having second thoughts.

"Why don't you two take a look around? I have a few things to do, but I'll catch up with you later. Here, you'll need this." He handed me a copy of the official programme.

It was difficult to read while holding on to Barry's lead, but I managed to find out where and when the 'mutt' competition would be held. On the inside cover of the programme was a full page tribute to Edna Vicars.

I signed Barry in, and locked him into one of the large cages which were provided.

"Let me out!" He did 'pathetic' really well.

"It's only for a few minutes. I'll be back soon."

Colonel Briggs had given me a list of the people who had been particularly close to Edna Vicars. Even though I felt sure that Maxwell would soon confirm Hector had been arrested and charged with his mother's murder, I didn't think it would do any harm to talk to her friends anyway.

Freda Giles was due to judge the terriers. She was a sprightly seventy year old with blue hair and a sharp tongue. "Edna was too set in her ways for me."

"How do you mean?"

"A judge should assess the dogs against the breed standard, and they shouldn't play favourites."

"Which group did she judge?"

"The Toy Group, always the Toy Group. Alistair Howard has had to step in to judge this year. You should talk to him. He knew Edna better than anyone."

I already had Alistair Howard on my list and tracked him down in the refreshment area, whiskey in hand.

"Just settling my nerves." He smiled.

"Feeling the pressure?"

"You can say that again. There's a lot of expectation now Edna—" he hesitated, a little embarrassed. "Now I've taken over."

"Expectation?"

"There are those who say that Edna had it in for certain breeds. Of course she denied it, and only she knew for sure, but it's true that no Pug or Papillon ever made it through to Best in Show while Edna was judging. Look, I'm sorry, but I have to prepare."

"Of course. Good luck."

With ten minutes to go until the start of the 'mutt' competition, my nerves were beginning to jangle. Barry showed no such stage fright. "Let's go!" He pulled on the lead.

"Not yet. We have to wait until it's our turn."

"What will I win?"

"Nothing most likely."

"What about a trophy?"

"Only for the winners. It isn't the winning, it's the taking part."

"Stuff that! I'm going to win. Just watch me."

When it was our turn, I walked slowly towards the ring. There was a surprisingly large crowd which greeted Barry enthusiastically. Me—they couldn't have cared less about. We'd watched the contestants who went before us, and to my surprise, Barry appeared to have been taking note. Instead of pulling me in ten different directions at once, which was what he usually did, he walked to heel. I could scarcely believe it. But it was the next part I was dreading. I had to undo Barry's lead, tell him to lie down, and then walk to the other side of the ring. So far, the dogs who had gone before us had behaved impeccably. They'd stayed put until called by their owners. The chances of Barry staying put were somewhere south of zero.

I unclipped the lead and gave him the command to lie down—he did. I was so stunned the judge had to prompt me to continue.

"Stay!" I said, with as much conviction as I could muster.

I turned my back on Barry, and began to walk across the ring. Any second now, he'd pounce on my back. Any second now.

I reached the other side, and turned to see Barry still lying where I'd left him.

On my command, he came running to me.

"How did you do that?" I said in a whisper.

"This stuff is easy. That trophy has my name on it."

# Chapter 17

Lester greeted us at Aunt Lucy's door. "Hi you two. Looks like someone had a good day."

"Third place." I held out the cup for Lester to see.

"Well done, Barry."

Barry huffed.

"What's wrong with him?" Lester beckoned us inside.

"He thinks he should have won."

"I was clearly the best." Barry paused to scratch himself.

"Maybe next time." Lester grinned at me.

"Where's Aunt Lucy?"

"There's been a bit of a mishap."

"Is she okay?"

"Yes, she's fine. It's just—"

"Look at this!" Aunt Lucy appeared from the bathroom. Her hair was lime green.

"Your hair is lime green." Sometimes I should just keep my big mouth shut.

"Thanks for that, Jill. I hadn't noticed."

"What happened?"

"Grandma happened."

"Why? How?"

"You may well ask. Apparently she holds me responsible for the actions of my daughters, and—" She glared at me. "The actions of my niece."

"You mean the hen night?"

"That's exactly what I mean. What were you thinking?"

"We'd had a lot to drink."

"So you thought you'd ditch Grandma? Surely you knew there would be repercussions?"

"I'm really sorry. If it's any consolation she gave us

the—"

"Please." She held up her hand. "I've already heard the grisly details from the girls. It serves the three of you right. Though why *I* should have to be punished, I don't know."

"Green does suit you," I said. Foot in mouth again.

"*Dark* green suits me," Aunt Lucy said. "I like my hair *dark* green. Not like this." She ran her hand through her hair. "Look at it!"

I sensed it was time to change the subject. "Barry took third place." I held up the trophy.

"Great! Maybe I can wear *that* on my head when I go to the wedding."

The moral of the story was clear: 'Do not cross Grandma.'

I left Barry and the trophy at Aunt Lucy's before driving back to Washbridge. It was on days like this I was pleased that I had two homes. I didn't envy the twins being stuck with Aunt Lucy and Grandma. I'd just have to give Ever a Wool Moment a wide berth for a few days.

Halfway home, I got a call from Kathy—could I go around straight away? What now? I was still feeling the after-effects of the hen night. All I really wanted to do was go to bed. Kathy was as insistent as she was mysterious.

"Surprise!" I was greeted with party poppers and silly string.

"What's this all about?"

"It's a thank you party for saving our holiday," Kathy said.

"Thanks, Auntie Jill." Lizzie threw her arms around me.

"Thanks, Auntie Jill!" Mikey threw a balloon which

bounced off my nose.

"A party? For me?" Oh goody. "You got the money back then?"

"The police returned it to us. Dominic Whitelaw had kept it at the power station. Looks like the holiday is back on."

"How's Norman Reeves doing?"

"He's okay." Kathy pulled silly string from her hair. "He's out of danger and might even be well enough to come on the holiday. He has a spare ticket, if you're interested?"

"I think I'll pass."

Peter was reading the kids their bedtime story.

"I don't understand why Dominic and Natasha did it," Kathy said. "Why would they kill someone for such a small amount of money?"

"It will all come out in court, but my guess is that originally they only ever intended to steal the money. Whitelaw had huge financial commitments and had lost his job. The redundancy money was never going to cover his outgoings. The holiday fund added up to a tidy sum. I guess they figured it was easy money that would keep them going until they had figured something else out."

"So why hurt Norman?"

"He must have caught them with the money, and threatened to go to the police. They panicked, and had no idea what to do, so they took him by force to the power station."

"They must have realised he was going to die?"

"Maybe, but more likely they just closed their eyes to the problem, and hoped it would go away. This wasn't a well planned crime. It was two very stupid people who tried to make a quick buck, and ended up in way over their heads."

"So Natasha deliberately set out to befriend Norman Reeves just to get to the money?"

"Yes, he was putty in her hands. Once she knew where he kept the cash, they took it, and that would have been an end to it if Norman hadn't found them out."

"The world is going crazy."

No arguments from me there.

"You look rough, Jill," Peter said, once the kids were down. "Are you okay?"

"You're such a charmer." Kathy slapped his arm. "He's right though, you do look off colour. Are you okay?"

"Just tired. I'm going to have to get off soon."

"Just wait until you've got kids," Kathy said. "Then you'll know what tired *really* is. Oh, and by the way, why was there a traffic warden in your car the other day?"

"It was just someone I used to know from school. I was giving her a lift."

"I don't remember her."

"You didn't know all of my friends."

"I did. There were only three of them."

"I had more than three friends." Four actually.

"What's her name? Your traffic warden friend?"

"Daisy Flowers."

Kathy laughed. "You've just made that up."

"That's her name, honestly. Everyone used to call her Daze."

"I still don't remember her."

"That's because you were too busy flashing your

knickers at all the boys in the playground."

"I did not flash my knickers."

"If they gave you a Snickers you did."

"Take no notice of her, Pete. She's lying. It was a Mars Bar."

Peter shook his head.

"I almost forgot," Kathy said. "Your aunt Lucy came around this morning."

I almost spat out the water I was drinking.

"She came here?"

"Yeah. She's lovely, isn't she? I'm not sure about the lime green hair though."

"Why did she come?"

"She invited us to visit her and the rest of your family in Malten next month."

"In Malten?"

"Yes."

"You're sure she said Malten?"

"Where else would she say? That's where she lives, isn't it?"

"Malten? Yes, of course, Malten. That's where Aunt Lucy lives."

"Are you sure you're okay, Jill?"

"Yeah, I'm just tired. I should be getting off."

Aunt Lucy had delivered on her promise. Somehow she'd used her magic to alter their memories—Kathy, Peter and the kids—so that they all now believed that my family lived in Malten, a small village thirty miles north of Washbridge. Did Aunt Lucy actually have a property in Malten? Oh well, at least now I didn't need to worry about Kathy asking about Candlefield.

It was the following day before my stomach was back to normal again.

"That isn't a scarf!" I said.

"I can see why you chose this profession." Mrs V stopped knitting. "Nothing gets past you, does it?"

"But you only ever knit scarves."

"Not any longer. I have set my sights on a second trophy."

"What is it? A hat?"

"A hat? Of course it's not a hat. It's a sock. The sock category is one of the toughest. Eva Doors has taken the trophy for the last seven years. But things are about to change."

"Good for you. Will you still knit the scarves?"

"Of course. I intend to defend my crown too."

"Going for the double then?"

"It's about time someone put Eva in her place. She's been getting a little—"

"Big for her socks?"

"Complacent."

My humour was wasted here.

"Good for you. Sock it to her."

What? Come on, that was funny.

"What are you wearing?" I asked Winky.

"The crazy old bag lady gave them to me." He held up a paw to show me one of the four red socks. "They're great for doing this." He took a few steps, and then slid across the floor. "Good eh?"

"Amazing. How's your love life?"

"I'm playing hard to get." He slid back across the floor.

"Is it working?"

"Early days. I've been offline for a couple of days. She's probably pining for me by now."

I glanced through the window. Bella was frantically waving her tiny flags around, but not in this direction.

"You'll ruin those socks." Mrs V was standing in the doorway, watching Winky slide from one side of the room to the other.

"He'll soon get bored with it," I said.

"I forgot to mention." Mrs V scowled as Winky slid past her. "Detective Maxwell called yesterday. He'd tried to get you on your phone, but you weren't answering. He'd like you to give him a call."

I did, and caught him on the first attempt.

"Can we meet?" he asked.

"Usual interview room?"

"Let's get a coffee for a change. Can you make it to Java's in fifteen minutes?"

"I'm going to meet Detective Maxwell for coffee."

Mrs V gave me a knowing look.

"What?"

"Nothing dear. Ask him what colour socks he'd like, will you?"

"You're a difficult person to get in touch with." Maxwell handed me a latte.

"Things have been a bit hectic."

"I promised I'd update you on the Vicars case." He took a bite of caramel shortbread.

"Have you charged Hector Vicars?"

He nodded—his mouth still full of shortbread. Eventually, he said, "Not with murder though."

"Manslaughter?"

"Armed robbery."

"What?"

"The car in the breaker's yard matched the one used in the recent bungled jewel robbery. We've arrested a man named Joseph Truman—better known as Battery."

"Hilary's boyfriend."

"We had him banged to rights, so he couldn't wait to cut a deal. He gave up your friend Hector Vicars as the getaway driver."

"What about the hit and run?"

"It couldn't have been Hector. He and Battery were busy bungling a jewel heist at the same time as Mrs Vicars was knocked down and killed."

I sighed. "Are you sure?"

"One hundred per cent positive. I don't know who knocked down Edna Vicars, but I do know it wasn't her son and it wasn't that car."

"Back to square one then."

"Looks like it."

"Oh, before I forget." I wiped the froth from my lips. "Mrs V wanted me to ask what colour socks you'd like."

"I thought she specialised in scarves?"

"She's branching out. Do you still have your Tweety Pie socks?"

He looked puzzled. "How did you know about those?"

"I'm a P.I.—remember? Why not have some red ones? They'll go with your bowling shirt."

He grinned, mopped up the last few crumbs of shortbread, and said, "I'll let you decide. You seem to have a lot to say about my fashion sense."

"Or lack of it."

As soon as we'd left the coffee shop, I contacted Colonel Briggs to ask if I could go over to see him. I wanted him to hear the news from me first.

"Jill, come in. I hear your boy, Barry, took third place."

"He thought he should have won first prize."

Colonel Briggs gave me a puzzled look.

"Err—I mean that's probably what he thought—I guess. Maybe."

"Is there any news on Edna's killer?"

"Hector Vicars definitely didn't kill his mother. He's been charged with robbery—a jeweller's shop. The raid took place at the same time as Mrs Vicars was killed, so he couldn't have been responsible. The police are still looking for the hit and run driver."

Colonel Briggs nodded. "Thanks for coming out here to tell me, and for all your efforts. Let me have your bill, and I'll see it is paid immediately."

"I'm sorry I couldn't help more than I did."

"You did everything you could. Now, will you stay for a drink?"

"I'm sorry, I can't. I just wanted to tell you the news face to face."

"Before you go. Take a look at these." He handed me a stack of photographs. "It's all the winners and runners-up. Your boy is among them."

Each photo showed a dog and its proud owner. On the back of each one, someone had written the name of the dog, and the owner. I flicked through them looking for the one with Barry and me, but it was another photo that caught my attention.

*'Free drink with every five balls of wool at Ever a Wool Moment!'* - the flyer read.

The man-sized balls of wool had once again taken over the high street. Grandma truly was a marketing machine. Perhaps I should ask her to handle publicity for my agency—but then again, perhaps not. I was about to cross the road to avoid being spotted when I heard her call my name.

"Jill! Sneaking off again, I see."

"Grandma. I was just—err—"

"Sneaking off, I know. Come in and have a drink."

"I'm rather busy—"

She shot me that look of hers—the one that threatened another few hours in the toilet.

"Okay, I guess I can spare a few minutes."

I'd assumed there would be free tea or coffee—maybe even a glass of wine. I hadn't anticipated the small bar that had been set up in the corner of the shop. Or the young man wearing only shorts and a smile who was busy shaking a cocktail while a crowd of old ladies ogled his six pack.

"That's Emilio," Grandma said. "What he doesn't know about cocktails isn't worth knowing."

"It appears to be a popular promotion."

"We've been run off our feet all day. What's your poison?"

Poison? I eyed her suspiciously. "Could I have a glass of water?"

"Emilio," Grandma shouted over the crowd. "A screwdriver for my granddaughter."

An hour later, I made my excuses and left, but only after I'd promised to tell Mrs V about Emilio and his cocktails.

# Chapter 18

The waiting room was busy. The man seated next to me had a streaming cold, but apparently no tissues. This was precisely why I hated going to see the doctor—I always ended up feeling worse. In one corner, two young children were playing with a selection of toy cars. Opposite me, a middle-aged man was telling the woman next to him all about his hernia—she looked suitably impressed. The woman at reception was run off her feet trying to cope with a steady stream of phone calls and patients, so she didn't notice I hadn't checked in. There were three doctors at the practice, and according to the illuminated board, two of them were on duty.

By ten to eleven, the waiting room was almost empty—just me, and a young man with a cast on his leg. After he'd seen the doctor, I started towards the surgery door.

"Excuse me," the woman called after me. I ignored her, and kept on walking until I found the door with Dr Mills' name on it.

"Hello?" He looked confused. "I thought I was done for the day." He checked his computer screen.

"I'm not one of your patients." I took a seat beside his desk.

"I'm sorry, you can't—"

"I'm here about Mrs Vicars."

"Edna?" Now I had his attention. "Are you a relative?"

"No. Let's just say I'm an interested party."

He shuffled nervously on his chair. "I'm not sure how I can help."

"I believe you were there when the hit and run happened?"

"Yes. I pronounced her dead."

"Why were you there?"

"I am—I was her doctor."

"According to her daughter she made regular visits to the surgery, but didn't have house-calls—Mrs Vicars said they were only for old people."

"She hadn't been feeling well."

"I believe all phone calls to the surgery are logged, so if I check back, will I find a call from Edna Vicars on that day?"

"I—err—I."

"Dr Mills, we both know the real reason why you went to see Edna that morning."

He could barely keep his hands still. "I don't know what you mean."

"You went there to try to persuade Edna Vicars to put your dog through to Best in Show. Did you offer her a bribe?"

He was silent for the longest moment, before beginning to crumble in front of my eyes. "It was an accident." He began to sob.

There was a knock on the door, and the receptionist appeared. "Dr Mills? Is everything okay?"

He managed to compose himself long enough to wave her away. "Everything's fine."

"What happened that morning?" I asked.

"Edna had it in for Pugs. I don't know why—they're such a wonderful breed. This was Benjy's last chance. He should have gone through to Best in Show last year, and the year before. He would have gone through if it had been any other judge, but not Edna. I tried to talk her round, and then—" he hesitated. "It was stupid. I don't know why I did it. I offered her money. It was stupid. So stupid."

"What did she do?"

"She said she'd report me. I told her no one would believe her—I told her I'd say she was delusional—that they'd lock her up. She was hysterical. I had to try to calm her down."

"Is that why she ran out of the house?"

"I wasn't going to hurt her. Just give her something to calm her down. I went after her, but then she stepped into the road—there was nothing I could do. I feel terrible. If I could only turn back the clock."

"So terrible that you went ahead with the competition anyway?"

"People would have asked questions if I hadn't."

"People are going to ask questions now. The police."

Thirty minutes later, they arrived to escort the doctor to the police station. He'd aged ten years during the course of the morning. I updated Maxwell on what I knew, and told him I thought the good doctor was ready to make a full statement.

What a stupid, needless tragedy. Edna Vicars lost her life because of a silly dog competition.

Daze had asked me to arrange to meet Damon Black, the rogue vampire, at Hotel Kromer. According to her, as soon as he sensed my blood type, the charm offensive would begin. I was worried that I might give the game away with a show of nerves. We'd arranged to meet in the lobby, and as soon as I spotted him I'd cast the 'doppelganger' spell, so he'd see me as the woman in my profile picture.

"Scarlet?"

"Huh? Oh, yes. Hi." Great start—I'd forgotten my own fake name.

"I'm Damon." The man was way too handsome for his own good. "Been waiting long?"

"No, not long."

"You're even more beautiful than your photograph." He flashed a smile.

Boy, this guy was good. If it wasn't for the fact he wanted to drain me of blood and leave me for dead, I could totally have gone for him.

"Thank you."

His eyes suddenly lit up, and something told me he'd registered my blood type.

"Shall we go through?" He took my arm; his hand was cold to the touch. "I'm ravenous."

But for what eh, buddy? Had he just glanced at my neck or was I being paranoid?

Everything Daze had told me about the man was true. His charm offensive was polished and relentless.

"Is your food all right?" he said, when he noticed me pushing it around the plate.

"It's lovely. I'm just not very hungry. Sorry."

"Another drink, maybe?"

"Just a little."

He'd insisted on ordering champagne—the most expensive on offer. Shame I had to feed it to the plant, but I wanted to keep my wits about me.

"Have I told you how beautiful you are?" He stared deep into my eyes.

"You have, but once more won't hurt." I giggled—got to make it look like the drink was starting to have an effect.

By the end of the meal, we were halfway down the second bottle of bubbly. The plant was well and truly inebriated, and I was doing a good impression of being tipsy.

"It's been a fantastic evening," he said. "Shame it has to end."

"It is," I agreed.

"I have a room here in the hotel. If you'd like a night cap?"

"You have a room?"

"I don't like to drink and drive."

"I really should go home."

"If that's what you want—"

He was good—very good.

"Just a nightcap?"

"Of course, and then I'll get you a cab."

"Okay. Just the one."

As we walked out of the restaurant, and through the lobby, I glanced around to see if I could spot Daze. Knowing her, she'd probably have taken a job at the hotel as cover.

As we made our way to his room, I could feel his gaze on my neck. I still hadn't seen Daze—maybe she was waiting in his room. He opened the door, stepped to one side and ushered me inside. Even though I could feel his presence behind me, it was a little unnerving to see only my reflection in the full length mirror next to the door. Where was Daze? I was beginning to get a little worried. If push came to shove, I could use my own magical powers, but I wasn't sure how well level one and two spells would fare against a determined vampire.

"That's a beautiful necklace," he said, as though he'd noticed it for the first time. "Let me see." He stooped—his face getting ever closer to my neck. Come on Daze. Where are you?

"That's close enough!" The squeaky voice made us both jump.

"Who are you?" Damon shouted.

A good question and one I wanted answering too. The diminutive young man with the squeaky voice certainly wasn't Daze unless she'd really upped her game when it came to disguises.

"Damon Black, you're under arrest." The young man was wearing a catsuit not dissimilar to the one worn by Daze. Whereas Daze cut an intimidating figure, Squeaky looked like his mother had bought him the costume for his tenth birthday. Where was Daze?

Damon pushed me aside, and started to walk towards Squeaky. "Step out of my way boy, before I crush you!"

"You are charged with violating the sup code of ethics!" Squeaky seemed unfazed by Damon's approach. He was either very brave or very, very stupid.

"Code of ethics? Don't make me laugh. Get out of my way now or—"

Everything happened so quickly, I barely had a chance to register what I'd seen. Damon had launched himself at Squeaky, who had sidestepped him with ease. A flash of light, just like that from the 'lightning bolt' spell, hit Damon in the back, sending him crashing into the wall. Before he could recover, Squeaky had employed the chain-link netting similar to the one that I'd seen Daze use.

"I'll be back," Squeaky said, and then the two of them

disappeared.

What on earth had just happened?

"Sorry about that." True to his word, Squeaky was back.

"What just happened?"

"Black's in custody. I'll process the paperwork later."

"But—who are you?"

"Sorry, I didn't get a chance to introduce myself. I'm Blaze, Daze's second in command."

"Daze and Blaze?"

"Catchy eh? That was my idea. Daze wanted me to call myself Link—my real name is Lincoln. I think Blaze works better, don't you?"

"Err—I—where is Daze?"

"She sends her apologies. She was double-booked—"

"Double-booked?"

"Yeah. That girl can kick some serious ass, but between you and me, when it comes to paperwork, she's a nightmare."

"So, are you a sup sup too?"

"Sup squared, that's me."

"I didn't think sups liked that term."

"Daze doesn't. I wouldn't advise using it around her. Me, I don't mind. Daze said she'll catch up with you soon. Thanks again for your help. I'd better get back and sort out the bad guy. See you around."

"Bye."

Winky was still playing hard to get with Bella.

"How's that working out for you?" I asked, as I poured milk into his bowl.

"I figure if I give it another two days, she'll be pining for me."

"Right." I didn't have the heart to tell him that Bella now appeared to be signalling to at least three other cats. "Where are your socks?"

"They made my paws sweat."

No one wants a cat with sweaty paws.

Mrs V popped her head into my office; she'd apparently given up on the intercom.

"There's a young woman to see you. She doesn't have an appointment."

"Name?"

"Hilary Vicars."

"Show her in."

"Will do, as soon as she has picked out a scarf."

"Of course."

"And socks."

"Naturally."

Hilary smiled, she looked much younger than the last time I'd seen her. Prettier too. She held up the scarf and socks by way of a question.

"Mrs V likes to knit."

"She has a lot of scarves."

"Not so many socks though. She's only recently moved on to those. Have a seat. You're looking much better than the last time we met."

"Thanks. I feel much better."

"What can I do for you?"

"I came to apologise really. I wasn't very helpful when you came to see me."

"Battery?"

She nodded. "Yeah, I was an idiot to ever go out with him. He was a friend of Hector's."

"Was he violent towards you?"

"Not physically, but he did scare me. I wanted to tell you about the car, but I couldn't. How did you find it?"

"I have my sources."

"Hector was livid. He'd told Battery to torch the car, but that big idiot tried to make a few quid by taking it to the breaker's yard."

"What are your plans now?" I asked.

"I'm going to move away. Maybe go abroad. There's nothing to keep me here now that Mum's gone. Somewhere Hector and Battery won't find me when they get out."

"Sounds like a plan."

"There's one thing I need to do before I leave. That's why I came to see you."

"What's that?"

"I know Mum wanted the Dog Rescue to have some of her money. She'd planned to change her Will. I'd like to donate some of the money I inherited."

"That's very generous, but you're under no obligation to do that. And besides, I didn't think you liked dogs?"

"I don't, but it's what Mum would have wanted. I wish I could donate Hector's share, but he'll no doubt blow that as soon as he gets out."

"Are you sure about this?"

"Positive."

"I can arrange a meeting for you with Colonel Briggs."

"No. Sorry. I don't want to see him."

"I'm sure he would like to thank you personally."

"No." She put the scarf and socks onto my desk while she fished around in her handbag. "Here." She handed me a cheque. "It's roughly a third. Would you give this to him please?"

My faith in human nature had almost been restored. If for every Hector there was a Hilary, maybe the human race would survive after all.

# Chapter 19

"I'm really not sure about this," I said, as I examined the line of socks strung across the outer office.

"I've run out of cupboard space," Mrs V said.

"Even so. I'm not sure it conveys the right impression."

"I thought it was rather Christmassy."

"Here's a crazy idea, why not take them home with you? And the scarves too?"

"That wouldn't work."

"Why not?"

"What would I give to your clients?"

"A friendly smile? A cup of tea?"

"Perhaps you could buy another cupboard for me to put the socks in?"

"Let me sleep on that."

Winky was on my desk—he didn't look up when I walked in.

"What have I told you about sitting on there?"

"Where is it?" His one good eye flitted back and forth as he looked around all corners of the room.

"Where is what?"

"It was over in that corner."

"What was? Will you get down off that desk!"

"Not until you get rid of that mouse."

"Mouse?" I climbed onto the leather sofa. I wasn't scared—I just didn't want to squash the poor little thing. "Are you sure you saw a mouse?"

"I suppose it could have been an Armadillo—of course I'm sure it was a mouse. Do you think I'm stupid?"

So tempted. "Why didn't you catch it then?"

He gave me a look of sheer contempt. "Catch it?"

"Isn't that what cats do?"

"I do not catch mice. I have far more important things to do with my time."

"Such as?"

"I read a lot. And I think. I spend a lot of time thinking."

"About what?"

"The meaning of life. Politics. Literature."

"Salmon?"

"Salmon too."

"I don't see it." I stepped down cautiously.

"You should call in an exterminator."

I was sorely tempted to do that, but not for the mouse problem.

"They cost money. Why have a dog and bark yourself?"

"What's that supposed to mean?"

"It means I have you."

"I'm not a dog."

"I know."

"Why do you want to bark?"

"Never mind. I don't have money for an exterminator. You'll have to get rid of it."

"I can't."

"Why not?"

He said something, but it was so quiet I didn't catch it. "Pardon?"

"I'm scared of mice, okay? Happy now that you've humiliated me?"

"I'm sorry."

"Then why are you laughing?"

"I'm not." I bit my lip. "I'm sorry. I didn't mean to—" I couldn't hold back the laughter another moment.

"I hate you." Winky turned his back on me.

On my way out of the office, I asked Mrs V if she'd call in an exterminator. She couldn't hide her disappointment when I explained it was actually for a mouse.

Daze had asked me to call in on her at the laundry. She was loading one of the industrial sized washing machines.

"Jill, hi."

"How many different jobs have you had?"

"I get bored easily." She closed the washing machine door, and pressed the 'wash' button. "The steam in here is playing havoc with my hair. Cup of tea?"

The tea came out of a vending machine at the back of the shop. The water in the washing machine would probably have tasted better.

"I wanted to apologise for the other day," Daze said. "I shouldn't have left you in the lurch like that. I'd double booked you with a werewolf money launderer."

"That's what your sidekick said. What's his name, 'Blaze'?"

"Yeah. Stupid name. What was he thinking? Daze and Blaze. We sound like a music hall act. I wanted him to be known as 'Link'. What do you think?"

I shrugged. The levels of surreal in my life still surprised me.

"How did he do?" she asked.

"I wasn't sure he'd be a match for Black, but he got the job done. The catsuit isn't a good look on him though."

"I've been telling him that for months, but I'm wasting my breath."

"Tomorrow's the big day!" Kathy screamed down the

phone.

"Yay!"

"You could at least try to sound excited. It *is* my birthday."

"I'm sorry. I am excited—honest. I'm just dead on my feet."

"Then get to bed. You have to be on top form tomorrow. You and I are going to get hammered."

The birthday tradition went back years. The rule was neither of us should work on our birthday, and we had to spend the whole day together. It was a bone of contention with Peter who felt Kathy should spend time with him and the kids on her birthday—I couldn't say I blamed him. But still the tradition continued. Normally, I was up for it, but this year I had the slight complication of a wedding on the same day.

"What time are we meeting?" I asked.

"You shouldn't have to ask. You know the drill. Usual time, usual place."

"Are you sure you want to meet at Barney's?"

"It's a tradition."

When we'd first started, Barney's had been one of *the* places to go to in Washbridge—it had been considered 'cool'. That was then. Now, it was a dive frequented by Washbridge's lowlife. The place made my skin crawl.

"Barney's it is then."

Colonel Briggs met me at the door to his house. "Where's your boy?"

"Barry? He's at home—polishing his trophy."

The colonel laughed. "And to what do I owe the pleasure?"

I brought him up to date with recent developments, in particular the arrest and confession of Dr Mills.

"I can't believe it. I never would have thought anyone would go to such lengths."

"A moment of madness, I think. I don't believe he intended to harm Mrs Vicars."

"What will happen to him?"

"That's up to the police and the Crown Prosecution Service. It's a difficult one to call."

"I feel terrible." The colonel sank into the chair.

"You couldn't have known about the doctor."

"It's not that. I feel terrible for blaming Edna's children. I had no right to point the finger at them."

"I wouldn't worry about it. Hector's a nasty piece of work. If you hadn't called me in, he might never have been brought to justice for the jewel robbery. Hilary turned out to be okay though. She's just escaped from a bad relationship, and is going to use some of the money she inherited to start a new life."

"Good for her."

"But she wanted you to have this." I handed him the cheque. He stared at it for a long moment.

"But why? Edna left the money to her."

"Hilary knows her mother planned to change her Will to leave the Dog Rescue some of her money. She thought it was the right thing to do under the circumstances."

"That's so very generous. Why didn't she come here herself so I could thank her?"

"I tried to persuade her to, but—well she asked if I'd do the honours."

"Thank you very much. I'm really grateful. Please give her my thanks."

"I will."

We talked for some time, mainly about Edna Vicars and the Dog Rescue. When it came time for me to leave, he walked me to the door.

"I apologise for the state of the gardens."

"They look beautiful."

"They're not up to the usual standard, I'm afraid. The grass needs a bit of a trim, and there are a few weeds peeping through. My gardener, Baxter, died recently. He'd been with me for nearly thirty years."

"I'm sorry."

"Good chap. Heck of a good chap. Still, comes to us all in the end, I suppose."

Winky was eating.

"Happy now?" I asked.

"I'd prefer salmon, but this will do I guess."

"I meant about the mouse."

Mrs V had insisted that the exterminator use a humane mouse trap, and that she accompany him to witness the mouse's release a safe distance from our offices.

"I don't know why you went to all that expense." Winky licked his lips. "I would have got rid of that little pest if you'd asked."

"You said you were scared."

"Don't be ridiculous. I'm a cat."

"You were the one who said I should bring in the exterminator."

"Have you been drinking the funny tea again?"

"Okay. If you're not scared of mice, you won't mind if I buy a couple from the pet shop. They can have the run of the office."

"Don't do that. They'll scare the clients."

# Chapter 20

The day of the wedding had arrived. Whoop-de-doo.

Have I mentioned I'm not a big fan of weddings? Kathy can't get enough of them. When and if I do get hitched, it'll be a quick trip to the Register Office for me.

I'd been told to report to Aunt Lucy's house—everyone was gathering there before going to the church.

"You two look gorgeous," I said. The twins were wearing matching pink, satin dresses. "I'm surprised that you didn't insist on having different colours."

"We tried to," Amber said. "Your mum wanted all three bridesmaids to wear the same colour."

"Right. That explains it. Wait a minute! What do you mean three?"

"Your dress is in Mum's bedroom."

"What do you mean *my* dress?"

"You'd better hurry. The cars will be here in twenty minutes."

"No one said anything to me about being a bridesmaid. I've never been a bridesmaid."

"Now's your chance." Aunt Lucy patted me on the shoulder, as she scurried by. I noticed her hair was back to its normal shade of dark green—if you could call dark green normal. Grandma must have taken pity and reversed the spell.

"Why didn't Mum tell me? She asked if I'd make a speech at the reception, but there was no mention of being a bridesmaid."

"Maybe she thought you wouldn't turn up." Pearl adjusted a shoulder strap on her dress.

She'd have been right. "What if it doesn't fit? I didn't go

for a fitting."

"Neither did we. The first time we saw ours was just before you arrived. Mum used a spell to create them—they're a perfect fit."

"But they're pink. I've never worn pink in my life."

"There's a first time for everything," Aunt Lucy called from the living room.

I stared at my reflection in the mirror—there was a whole lot of pink going on. I couldn't fault the fit—more's the pity. I could have killed my mother. The problem was she was already dead.

"Jill!" Amber called from downstairs. "Come down. We want to see."

"Yeah, come and give us a twirl," Pearl shouted.

Someone was going to pay for this.

"You look so pretty," Amber said, barely stifling a laugh.

"In pink," Pearl said, and then the two of them collapsed into giggles.

"Ha, ha. Very funny."

"Ignore them." Aunt Lucy looked me up and down. "You look fantastic. Your mother will be so proud."

"What on earth are you wearing?" Kathy's jaw dropped.

My juggling act with the wedding and Kathy's birthday hadn't got off to a great start. "I've had it ages." I tried to ignore the looks from the other customers in Barney's.

"It's pink."

"Light red."

"It's a joke, right?"

"What's wrong with it?"

"You look like you should be going ballroom dancing or to a wedding."

"I like it."

Kathy shook her head in disbelief. "What do you want to drink?"

"Coke please."

"You're not drinking coke on my birthday. You know the rules. Beer or spirits."

"I'll have the same as you."

"Half a lager," Kathy called to the barman.

"Coming right up. Is it for you or the sugar plum fairy?"

Everyone's a comedian.

"Mother," Aunt Lucy shouted. "You are *not* wearing that!"

While I'd been with Kathy, Grandma had arrived. She and Aunt Lucy were in the living room.

The twins were peeping through the open door, doing their best not to laugh.

"What's happening?" I mouthed.

Pearl beckoned me closer. "Look," she whispered.

"What's wrong with it?" Grandma said.

"It's a wedding dress!"

"Well? Are we or are we not going to a wedding?"

"Not yours! You can't turn up to Darlene's wedding wearing a wedding dress."

Grandma did a twirl.

"Where did she get it from?" I whispered. "Is it the one she got married in?"

"No." Pearl shook her head. "That must have perished

centuries ago. She bought it from a charity shop close to Ever a Wool Moment."

"Why?"

Amber laughed. "Because she's nutty as a fruit cake."

"Go and get changed!" Aunt Lucy shouted. "Or you're not going!"

Grandma huffed and puffed, but in the end relented.

"Is Mum travelling with us?" I asked, after Grandma had left.

"No." Aunt Lucy still looked exasperated after her run-in with Grandma. "She's going to meet us at the church."

"Where did you go?" Kathy said. "One minute you were there and the next you'd gone."

"I needed the loo."

"Are you actually going to drink that or just stare at it all day?"

"Sorry." I'd been hoping to pour the lager into the nearby potted plant, but Kathy was watching me like a hawk.

"We need shots." Kathy banged on the counter. "Two shots, bartender."

"Isn't it a bit early for—" I began.

"Shots for the sugar plum fairy and her friend coming right up." He grinned.

"Jill?" Amber looked flustered. "Where have you been? I've been looking for you everywhere."

I hadn't told any of my Candlefield family about Kathy's birthday. I didn't want them to think that I wasn't giving the wedding my full attention.

"Here!" She handed me a small bouquet of pink and

white carnations. "Come on, the cars are outside."

"Coming."

Outside were two white limos. In the first car were Grandma, Aunt Lucy and Lester. In the second one were Pearl, Alan and William. I began to follow Amber towards the second car.

"Jill!" Grandma yelled. "You're travelling with us."

Great. I glanced at the twins who were doing a poor job of hiding their amusement.

"I thought I'd ride with the twins."

"You thought wrong." Grandma patted the seat beside her. "Get in."

Grandma had changed into a red and black dress which was more 'Halloween' than 'wedding day'. Aunt Lucy saw me staring at Grandma's dress, and rolled her eyes.

"Have you been drinking?" Grandma put her face closer to mine. I shuffled along the bench seat.

"No."

"Are you sure? It smells like beer to me."

"I took some medicine." I coughed. "Tickly throat."

"Hmm." Grandma wasn't buying it.

The drive to the church took less than five minutes.

Everyone except Amber, Pearl and me had made their way into the church.

"How's Mum getting here?" I said, looking back towards the gate.

"I'm already here."

I turned around to find my mother dressed all in white.

"You look beautiful," I said. She really did.

"Thank you, dear. You too. I hope you like pink."

I forced a smile, and then turned to the twins. "Don't

you think she looks fantastic?"

They shrugged. How rude.

"They can't see me," Mum said. "You're the only one who can see me while we're out here."

"What about in the church?"

"Grandma has cast a spell that will allow everyone to see us for the duration of the ceremony. It's an incredibly complicated, level six spell, and will only last for a short time. She's going to do the same at the reception during the speeches."

Speech—I'd been trying to forget about that. I still hadn't got anything down on paper.

The organist began to play the wedding march.

"Ready?" Mum asked.

I nodded, and we fell in behind her. Aunt Lucy was waiting just inside the doors. She took my mother's arm and led her down the aisle—three visions in pink following behind. Alberto, dressed in an immaculate, black designer suit, turned to see his bride. It had just occurred to me that he was about to become my stepfather—a ghost stepfather. Drake and his killer smile were seated next to Alan and William in the second row.

The twins and I followed Aunt Lucy to the front pews, and the ceremony began. Aunt Lucy was the first to cry, followed by the twins. My eyes may have watered a little, but then it was dusty in the church—I totally didn't cry.

"Why do you keep disappearing?" Kathy knocked back another shot.

"I nipped out to get you these." I handed her my bouquet.

"Err—thanks. Where did—?"

"Do you like them?"

"Err—yes, thank you." She rubbed her head—probably beginning to doubt her own sanity. Or mine. "Drink up. Time to move on."

I pretended to reach for the shot, but accidentally on purpose knocked it over. "Whoops."

"Come on, clumsy. Let's find somewhere a bit more lively."

That shouldn't be difficult.

"Jill?" Pearl shouted. "Where have you been? We've been looking for you everywhere."

"Sorry. I was feeling a little light-headed," I lied. "I took a walk to clear my head. Where is everyone?"

"They've gone to the reception. We're going home first to get changed."

"Good idea." Anything to get out of this pink horror.

The three of us split up. The twins made their way back to their place where the outfits they'd purchased especially for the evening reception, were waiting for them. I headed to Aunt Lucy's to get changed back into the clothes I'd arrived in—the ones I'd expected to wear all day.

"Jill!" said Kathy. We were in Liberty's, an altogether different proposition to Barney's. Liberty's was the newest, sparkiest bar in town. "What's wrong with you? You were miles away."

"Sorry, must be the drink."

"Speaking of which, I need a cocktail. What shall we have?"

"I think I'll stick with the lager."

"No you won't. Don't you know what time it is?"

I was about to check my watch when she screamed, "It's cocktail time!"

Oh boy.

Aunt Lucy's front door was ajar. Had she come back too? "Hello? Aunt Lucy?"

I'd no sooner stepped inside than I was knocked to the ground by two figures who were headed for the door. Two hooded figures—Followers.

"Stop!" I screamed after them. As though that was going to work.

By the time I got to my feet and out of the door, they'd disappeared. Even if I'd seen which way they'd gone, I wasn't exactly dressed to give chase. What had they been doing in the house? Had they been looking for something? I looked around—upstairs and down—there was no sign of any disruption. Had they been looking for me? If so, why run off like that? Should I tell Aunt Lucy?

I got changed, and checked my reflection in the mirror—it was good to be back in my own clothes.

Back in Washbridge, Kathy stared at me.

"What?"

She continued to stare, and then I realised.

"What happened to the pink dress? How did you—?"

I was never going to talk my way out of this one, so I cast the 'sleep' spell. I caught Kathy in my arms, and asked one of the security men to help me to get her to the taxi.

"Back already?" Peter looked at his watch. "This must be some kind of record."

"She was hitting the shots pretty hard."

Between the two of us, we managed to get Kathy into bed.

"What about you?" Peter asked once we'd crept out of the bedroom. "You still look sober."

"I'm a bit merry," I faked. "I'll take the cab home. Tell her 'happy birthday' when she wakes up. Oh, and these are hers." I handed him what was left of the bouquet, which Kathy had sat on during the cab drive home.

Back at Aunt Lucy's, I heard a noise coming from downstairs. Someone was in the house. Had the Followers come back?

I crept slowly down the stairs. It was silent—had I imagined it? I peered into the living room—nothing. I edged my way towards the kitchen—ready to cast the 'lightning bolt' spell. Nothing there either. I must have imagined it.

A hand touched my arm; I spun around.

"Drake?"

"Are you okay?"

"What are you doing here?"

"The twins came back without you. I was beginning to worry."

"I'm fine."

"Are you sure?"

"Yeah. I'll go and get my shoes."

The reception was at the Candlefield Hotel. The exterior wasn't very promising—a lick of paint was well overdue—but the interior more than made up for it. The ballroom was huge and beautifully decorated.

My mother looked even more breathtaking close up. "You look stunning," I said.

"Thank you. I couldn't have wished for prettier bridesmaids. Did you like the dress?"

"Err—yes—it was very—err. Pink."

"My favourite colour."

"Hmm."

"Do you have your speech ready?"

"Speech? Yes. All ready."

"I'm looking forward to hearing it. I suppose I'd better circulate. Catch you later."

# Chapter 21

Someone tapped on a wine glass and the room fell silent. The meal had looked delicious, but I hadn't been able to eat more than a few mouthfuls. I was too busy worrying about the speech—the one I hadn't got around to writing. I was seated at the top table between my mother and Aunt Lucy. The twins were seated to my right.

All eyes were on me when I stood up. Drake, who was sitting with Lester, William and Alan, gave me an encouraging thumbs-up—it didn't help.

"Ladies—" My voice cracked, so I took a sip of water. "Ladies and gentlemen. We are here today to celebrate the marriage of my mother, Darlene, to Alberto. Until a few weeks ago, I'd never met my birth mother. I was raised by my adoptive parents as a human, so you can imagine my surprise when I found out that I was actually a witch."

There was a smattering of polite laughter.

"I'd always assumed that my mother had abandoned me, but I now know that she has always been by my side—I just couldn't see her. I feel truly blessed to have been re-united with her—even if I did have to wait until after she was dead."

A little more polite laughter.

"Discovering who I was, after all of those years came as something of a shock as you can imagine. But I can honestly say that it is, without a doubt, one of the best things that has ever happened to me. I now have a whole new family who, until recently, I didn't even know existed."

The twins beamed at me.

"I'm grateful for the opportunity to be here today, to witness my mother's joy at getting married to Alberto, her childhood sweetheart. Has there ever been a more beautiful bride?"

Everyone cheered and clapped. Can ghosts blush? I felt sure I saw my mother's cheeks colour.

"Or such a dashing groom as Alberto?"

More cheers and applause.

"Please be upstanding and join me in a toast."

Everyone, even Grandma, got to their feet.

"The bride and groom!"

My mother took my hand, squeezed it, and mouthed the words, "Thank you."

"I need a drink," I joined Drake at his table.

"Great speech." He poured me a glass of champagne.

"Was it okay? I had intended to prepare something."

The twins grabbed two chairs from an adjoining table, and squeezed in next to their respective partners.

"It was brilliant." Amber took a sip from William's glass.

"I'm glad I didn't have to make a speech." Pearl gave Alan a peck on the cheek.

Thirty minutes later, the tables had been moved to the edge of the room. On the small stage, a four piece band struck up. Within moments, the dance floor was full. Amber and Pearl were really going for it.

"Want to dance?" Drake held out his hand.

"I've got two left feet."

"That's okay. I have two right ones. We'll cancel each other out."

The first number, which I'd never heard before, had a fast tempo. Kathy always said that I danced like a drunken windmill. Drake didn't seem to mind.

Three hours later, and I was really getting into the groove. Or maybe it was just the drink. Either way, I was having a great time. My only disappointment was that human music didn't seem to have made it to Candlefield.

"Grandma's leaving." Aunt Lucy tapped me on the shoulder.

"It is getting late," I said, trying to be heard over the sound of the band.

"For you, maybe, young lady."

Grandma was behind me—I should have known.

"This is too lame for me," she said. "I'm going clubbing. Care to come?"

"Err—thanks, but—I don't think so."

"You youngsters. No staying power." With that, she was gone.

Aunt Lucy shrugged resignedly.

Drake and I were all danced out.

"Who exactly was the man I saw you with in Washbridge?" he said.

Since the awkward encounter between Drake and Jack Maxwell, neither man had enquired about the other. I was beginning to think that neither of them would.

"Maxwell. Detective Jack Maxwell."

"So, it was business then?"

"Not exactly. I won a charity raffle, or at least my sister fixed it so that I won. The date with Detective Jack Maxwell was the prize."

"So, not a real date?"

"Not really."

"Good—I mean, I see."

"Jill, we're going home now." Aunt Lucy and the twins looked dead on their feet.

"Where are the guys?"

"They've taken a cab."

"William is drunk." Amber did not look happy.

"Alan is even more drunk," Pearl said.

"I'm pretty sure Lester was drunker than both of them," Aunt Lucy chimed in.

"Men!"

Those three men would be in for a hard time in the morning.

"Are you coming, Jill?" Aunt Lucy said.

"I'd better get off," I said to Drake. "I'm ten kinds of shattered."

"Okay. Maybe I'll see you again soon."

"Ooooh!" The twins chorused.

I shot them a look, and then turned back to Drake. "Sure. I'd like that."

We all went back to Aunt Lucy's. The twins and I were going to share their old bedroom. No sleep for me then.

"My throat feels like a mouse crawled into it and died." Amber coughed. "Do you have anything to drink, Mum?"

"No more alcohol for you three tonight!"

"I meant lemonade or coke."

"There's coke in the fridge."

"So, Jill?" Amber said, as she opened the fridge. "What about Drake?"

"What about him?"

"He seems—"

A cloud of yellow smoke began to fill the kitchen.

"What's going on?" Aunt Lucy screamed. "Girls? Are you okay?"

"I'm okay," I said.

"Me too." Pearl coughed.

The smoke had almost dissipated now. The fridge door was open, but there was no sign of Amber.

"Amber?" Aunt Lucy shouted. "Where are you? Don't mess around, this isn't funny."

Pearl and I exchanged a look. Instinctively, I knew this wasn't a joke.

Ten minutes later, after the three of us had searched the house and garden; there was still no sign of Amber.

"I have to get Grandma," Aunt Lucy said. "She'll know what to do."

"Wait!" I called. "There's something I need to tell you first."

"It'll have to wait, Jill. I need—"

"There were Followers in the house."

Aunt Lucy stared at me with eyes full of dread. "When?"

"When I came back to get changed. They ran away as soon as I got here."

"Why didn't you say something?"

"I—err—I didn't want to spoil the day—I'm sorry, I should have told you."

"Never mind, I need to get Grandma."

The knock on the door stopped us all in our tracks. Aunt Lucy rushed over and pulled it open.

"Amber!" Aunt Lucy threw her arms around her

daughter. "Are you okay?"

Amber didn't look particularly okay—she looked as though she'd just woken from a deep sleep.

"What happened?" Amber said.

"Don't you remember?" Pearl hugged her sister.

Amber shook her head. "I was getting coke out of the fridge."

"What's that?" I pointed to something sticking out of Amber's pocket.

Aunt Lucy took the envelope, tore it open, and stared at the small slip of paper.

*'Daughter of Darlene, be warned. I can take you or any of your family any time I please.'*

To my surprise, the twins were soon in their beds and sleeping like logs. I was too upset and angry to sleep. Aunt Lucy had found Grandma, and brought her back to the house. The three of us were now at the kitchen table.

"We have to do something about this," I said.

Grandma gave me an icy stare. "We? And what exactly does a level two witch think she can do against the Dark One?"

"I don't know, but surely we have to try to do something."

"Don't you think that others have already *tried*?"

"I—err."

"Sups much more powerful than you have tried and failed."

"But we don't even know who he is or what he is. What are the local police doing?"

"This isn't really their field."

"What do they do then?"

"That's a good question."

"What about sup sups, like Daze? Why don't they go after the Dark One?"

"What makes you think they aren't doing? You've only been here for five minutes. You have no idea what goes on."

That had put me firmly in my place. There was no arguing with Grandma while she was in this mood. I let it go, made my excuses, and crawled into the sleeping bag in the twins' bedroom. But this was far from over. The Dark One had crossed a line tonight, and I wasn't about to let it lie.

The twins were still fast asleep when I got up the next morning. Grandma and Aunt Lucy were at the kitchen table. Had either of them been to bed?

"Toast?" Aunt Lucy stood up when she saw me.

"No thanks. I'll just have a little cereal."

"Sit down." Grandma pointed to the chair opposite to hers.

"I thought I'd take my breakfast upstairs."

"Sit down!"

"Or maybe, I'll eat it here. That would work as well."

"Where did you get that smart mouth from?" Grandma was eating something that resembled frog spawn.

Aunt Lucy put the cereal on the table, stooped, and whispered in my ear. "Take no notice of grumpy."

"You're not too old to be turned into a snail," Grandma told Aunt Lucy.

"Cut the girl some slack." Aunt Lucy glared at her mother. "She's only known she was a witch for five minutes."

"All the more reason not to go shouting her mouth off with wild threats that she can't back up."

"She's Darlene's daughter! Your granddaughter! What do you expect?"

"I expect her to pack up that silly human job of hers, and move to Candlefield where we can protect her."

"Not happening!" I banged my spoon onto the table. "I was right here, in Candlefield, last night, but it didn't do much good did it?"

"What's going on?" Amber covered a yawn.

"What's all the noise about?" Pearl said, and then she spotted Grandma. "Sorry."

"Your cousin has decided to move to Candlefield permanently," Grandma said.

"No I haven't." I stormed past the twins. Thirty minutes later, I'd showered and dressed.

"Don't let Grandma get to you." Aunt Lucy put a hand on my shoulder. "She means well."

"I'm not leaving Washbridge," I said.

"I'll tell Grandma you need more time to consider it."

"You can tell Grandma to go take a running jump."

I was still seething when I arrived back at my flat. The cheek of the woman. Telling me to leave Washbridge when she'd just set up a shop there. NEVER GOING TO HAPPEN!

I would speak to Daze. If anyone could find out who or what the Dark One was, surely it would be the sup sups. And anyway, she owed me a favour for helping to catch Damon Black.

"Oh, Ivy!" A woman's voice caught my attention.

Just what I needed. I glanced down the corridor. Mr Ivers' latest conquest was a brunette. A little older than DeeDee, but apparently with the same MENSA rating. "You're so naughty, Ivy!"

Give me strength. I couldn't take any more of Ivy and his harem. Maybe it was time I checked out what was happening at speed dating. The whole concept sounded rather weird to me. It was hard enough trying to get to know someone when you had the whole night. How were you meant to do it in five minutes? I'd spent longer than that talking to the barista while he made my coffee.

# Chapter 22

"Morning, Jill." Mrs V gave me the same disapproving look every time I brought in coffee.

"Morning, Mrs V."

"There's perfectly good coffee in the jar. I don't know why you waste your money on that stuff. And what's that behind your back?"

How did she do that? I swear the woman had X-ray vision.

"Just a snack."

"Another blueberry muffin?"

"Only a small one."

Another disapproving look—I didn't care. After the wedding and its aftermath, I deserved blueberries, and if they happened to come wrapped in a muffin, who was I to argue?

"What's that you're knitting?" Notice the subtle change of subject? A master at work.

"It's a scarf."

"I thought you'd moved on to socks."

"I have, but I'm taking part in the scarf-a-thon. I thought you'd have heard about it."

"I'm not really up on yarn news and events."

"Your grandmother organised it."

"She never mentioned it. What is it exactly?"

"Everyone who takes part has twenty four hours to knit a scarf that must be one hundred stitches wide. The sponsors pay so much for every inch of the finished scarf. All proceeds go to charity."

"That sounds like a great idea. How long are you hoping for?"

"I'm not sure, but don't worry, it won't bankrupt you."

"Me?"

"Your grandmother put you down as a sponsor."

"That was kind of her."

"I told her I thought two pounds an inch was too much, but she insisted you'd want to pledge at least that amount."

"That's great." I took a bite of muffin. "Just great."

"Where's mine?" Winky asked, one-eyeing my muffin.

"Cats don't eat muffins."

"This one doesn't—apparently. Because someone is too mean to buy him one."

"I feed you. You should be grateful."

"How would you like it, if you had to eat cat food for breakfast, lunch and dinner?"

"I'm not a cat."

"Are you really going to eat all of that by yourself?"

"It's only a small one." I stuffed the rest into my mouth.

"Animal cruelty—I have a good mind to report you."

My phone rang.

"Jill?"

My mouth was otherwise engaged with blueberry muffin.

"Jill? Are you there?"

If I choked to death, it would be Kathy's fault. Cause of death—blueberry muffin asphyxia.

"Jill?"

"I'm here. Sorry, I was—"

"Stuffing your face by the sound of it. Are you back on the muffins?"

"It was only a *small* one. You sound rough."

"No kidding. My head feels like it's about to explode. What did I drink yesterday?"

"What *didn't* you drink?"

"What about you? How do you feel this morning? Pete said you seemed sober when you brought me home."

"Sober? He must be joking. I'm feeling pretty rough too. That's why I had the muffin—best cure ever for a hangover."

"I must have been really out of it." Kathy coughed, and sounded for a moment like she might throw up. "I can't remember very much at all, but I keep getting this image of you wearing a pink dress. Like a bridesmaid."

"Pink dress? Me? You must have been hallucinating."

"So you weren't wearing a pink dress?"

"Course not. Sounds like you should go back to bed."

"I'm going to, but I need a favour."

When didn't she?

"I've got a dentist appointment this afternoon. Pete's at work. Is there any chance you could collect the kids from school, and stay with them at my place until I get home?"

"Sure, no problem." It was the least I could do after wrecking her birthday. "Are you sure you can face the dentist with that hangover?"

"Not really. Hopefully I can sleep it off before then. I'm going back to bed. See you later."

"Later."

I should have felt guilty about casting a 'sleep' spell on my sister, and then lying to her. I should have, but I didn't. It was payback for stealing my beanies, and for all those terrible blind dates she'd set me up on. Revenge was sweet—sweet as a blueberry muffin.

I spent the next two hours catching up on paperwork,

and ignoring Winky's jibes. If he wanted a muffin, he'd have to bake his own.

I heard the outer door open.
"Who's that?" I wondered aloud. I knew I didn't have any appointments scheduled.
"Maybe it's the muffin man," Winky said.
It wasn't.
"Detective Maxwell is here," Mrs V said, with a silly grin on her face. "Shall I show him in?"
"Only if he has muffins," Winky meowed.
"Yes, please." I turned to Winky. "You! Behave or else."
"Do I get a muffin if I do?"
"Maybe."
"Chocolate chip?"
"Jill," Maxwell had had his hair cropped short.
"Morning. Nice haircut."
"Do you like it?"
"The convict look suits you. Grab a seat."
"Your receptionist didn't try to give me a scarf today."
"That's good."
"She got me to sponsor her instead."
"Oh. Sorry about that."
"It's for a good cause, I guess. I said I'd match whatever you were sponsoring her."
"Are you sure? Two pounds?"
"Why not? Two pounds a foot—how much can it cost me?"
"An inch."
"What?"
"It's two pounds an inch." I laughed.
"Whoops. Oh well, there goes my beer money for the

month."

Probably for the year. "What brings you here?"

"I was passing, and I wanted to give you an update on the Vicars case before the press get a hold of it."

"Thanks."

"No charges are going to be brought against Doctor Mills. The CPS decided it wasn't in the public interest, and to be honest, I agree with them. His only crime was trying to persuade Mrs Vicars she shouldn't discriminate against his dog. There's no evidence he actually threatened her—although she obviously felt afraid, which is why she rushed out of the house, and into the path of the car."

"He tried to bribe her."

"Maybe, but that's an issue for the organisers of the dog show. They may decide to strip him of his title, but it isn't a police matter."

"If he hadn't gone around to see her, she might still be alive."

"Again, that's true, but what would we charge him with?"

"So he just walks free?"

"It looks that way, but my guess is he'll punish himself for the rest of his life. He knows he was at least partially to blame. I doubt he'll practise medicine again—he'll probably retire."

"What about the car?"

"We're still looking for it. I'm not sure if we'll ever find it."

"Okay, well thanks for letting me know. I'll update Colonel Briggs."

"I don't suppose you fancy a drink tonight?" Maxwell said, as he stood up to leave.

"I can't, I'm sorry." Damn that speed dating. "Maybe another time?"

"Sure."

"Maxwell just asked me out," I said to Winky after he'd had left.

"Do I look like I care? Don't forget you promised to buy me a chocolate chip muffin. Make that double chocolate."

The teacher on the gate checked my ID as I entered the playground—Kathy had notified them that I'd be collecting the kids. Security was tighter there than at the local police station.

I think I'd rather face an armed robber than have to do the school run regularly. Those mothers were all crazy. Different factions seemed to occupy separate areas of the school yard. I was standing all alone, attracting suspicious glances from all sides. I smiled and said 'hello' to a couple of the women as they walked by. Neither smiled back. Neither spoke. How did Kathy cope?

A bell rang, and the kids came running out.

"Auntie Jill!" Mikey screamed.

"Auntie Jill!" Lizzie threw her arms around me.

"Hi guys. How was school?"

"I made a skelington," Lizzie said. "They only have bones. No skin."

"It's skeleton," Mikey said.

"That's what I said, silly."

"What about you, Mikey? What did you do?" I said.

"We did clouds and rain."

"Was it interesting?"

"Not really. I like cars better."

The kids insisted that they always had a bar of chocolate and a bottle of pop when they got home from school. I went along with it even though I suspected I was being played. When she got back from the dentist, Kathy would probably kill me for letting them have so much sugar.

"I see you still have the bion," I said. The frankensteinesque beanie that Kathy had made for Lizzie gave me the creeps. Why ruin two perfectly good beanies to create that monstrosity? And what were you supposed to catalogue it under? Bear? Lion? Freak-show?

"Mum's going to make me a giraphant soon."

"Giraphant? Let me guess—"

"It's a giraffe's head and neck on an elephant's body."

"Nice." What was wrong with this family? My poor little beanies.

"Beanies are stupid!" Mikey said matter-of-factly.

"They're better than stupid cars," Lizzie countered.

This was beginning to feel like a day out with the twins.

"Beanies and cars are both nice." I played the diplomacy card. I knew how to handle kids.

"Cars smell!"

"Do not!"

"Do so!"

"Beanies smell more!"

"Do not!"

"Do too!"

Scrub that. I was clueless when it came to kids.

I had hoped the three of us might play a game together, but it quickly became apparent that there was no common ground between the two kids. Instead, I split my time between the two of them. The first half hour I spent with Mikey, when I endured cars crashing against my feet and ankles. That was fun!

As a kid, I'd never had a dolls' house of my own—I'd had to share one with Kathy. You can imagine how that went. Lizzie's dolls' house was beautiful.

"Can we play outside?" Lizzie said.

"Does Mummy let you take the dolls' house into the garden?"

"Oh yes. Can we?"

It was a beautiful day, so why not? I lifted the dolls' house carefully—I didn't want a repeat performance of the Lego hotel affair. Mikey joined us in the garden, but gave us and the dolls' house a wide berth. He occupied himself with throwing stones at his action figures.

Lizzie had accumulated an incredible collection of furniture for her dolls' house, but I was disappointed to see that she shared her mother's bad taste in home furnishings. Lizzie was obviously very proud of it, and insisted on talking me through each and every item of furniture. Being the good auntie that I was, I did my best to stay awake.

"This is my new one." Lizzie handed me a tiny kettle. "It's blue. It's my favourite."

She was just like her mother. Kathy loved buying new stuff—anything, as long as it was new.

"Kids!" Kathy shouted. She'd arrived home just in time. Another five minutes, and I'd have been comatose with boredom. Mikey and Lizzie sprinted into the house. My legs had gone dead, so I struggled to my feet.

It was like it happened in slow motion. The tiny kettle slipped from my hand and bounced once, then twice and then a third time, before disappearing into the grate.

No! This couldn't be happening!

The good news was that it had landed on a small ledge just above the water line. The bad news was that it was too far down for me to reach with my fingers.

I had to focus. On the last occasion I'd used the 'shrink' spell, my clothes hadn't shrunk with me, and I'd ended up naked. When I'd discussed this with my mum, she'd said I needed to focus more on the desired outcome. I cast the spell, and to my relief, it worked just as I'd intended. This time my clothes had shrunk along with me.

It was an awful long way down to the ledge, but there were lots of weeds to grab hold of. All I had to do was—aaaaghh!

I managed to grab the stalk just in time. Phew, that was a close call—I'd almost ended up in the water. I clasped the weed with both my arms and legs, and slid slowly down until my feet touched the ledge.

"Jill?" Kathy's voice echoed around the chamber. "Jill? Where's Auntie Jill, kids?"

"She was here," Lizzie said.

"Maybe she's gone to the loo."

I waited until the voices had disappeared, before climbing back up the weed. It wasn't easy because I was holding onto the kettle at the same time.

I was lying on the ground, exhausted, when I saw the bird swooping down towards me. I was about to become his dinner. I reversed the spell just in time, scaring the poor bird to death.

"Jill? We've been looking everywhere for you," Kathy said. "Where have you been?"

"I just nipped to my car. How did it go at the dentist?"

Kathy stared at me—she sensed something was amiss.

"I was admiring Lizzie's kettle." I held it up. "She has the same bad taste as you."

# Chapter 23

I blamed Mr Ivers. If it hadn't been for his inexplicable transformation into 'Ivy' I would have been having a drink with Jack Maxwell. Would that have been our first, second or third date? The raffle prize probably didn't count, and the bowling had been no more than a ruse to humiliate me. So maybe it would have been our first ever *proper* date.

I'd had to turn down his offer of drinks because speed dating only took place on one night each week, and I'd already booked my place — under a false name, obviously. Lottie Levine — I thought the name suited me.

Who knew speed dating would be so popular? The ballroom of the Regent Hotel was full of small tables. The women were already seated; I'd been allocated table thirty six, which was near to the cloakroom. At the far end of the room was a small posse of men. I felt strangely nervous.

A bell rang, and the men hurried like mice through a maze until they found their first 'date'.

"Hello, I'm Walter," Walter said. That's all he said. Either he was the most nervous person on the planet or he really didn't like me. I tried a few times to start a conversation, but I only managed to extract two smiles and one raised eyebrow.

"Bye," he said when the bell rang again.

"Hi, sexy. I'm the man you've been waiting for all of your life," the next man said.

Come back Walter. All is forgiven.

Leo talked a good game, but I had my suspicions that if any woman actually responded to his ludicrous lines, he'd probably run a mile. I didn't test my hypothesis, just in case I was wrong.

The bell rang.

"I like trains."

"Really?"

"My name is Timothy. Do you like trains?"

Who knew five minutes could last so long?

The bell rang.

"Lottie? It suits you."

"Jack?"

"Arnold, please." Jack Maxwell pointed to his name badge.

"Arnold?" I laughed. "Do me a favour."

"It's not as bad as Lottie. Where did you come up with that?"

I shrugged.

"So," he said. "This is why you wouldn't come out for drinks?"

"I'm here on a case."

"Of course you are."

"It's true. Anyhow, what about you?"

"Same."

"You're a liar." I adjusted my name badge. "How did you know I'd be here?"

"You should know the answer to that by now."

"Because you're a detective."

"Correct. So, what do you think? Are we a match?"

"You're better than some I've met tonight."

"High praise indeed," he said. "So how about we arrange to do something another night?"

"I could whup your ass at bowling again. That was fun."

"No thanks. How about the movies?"

"Not my thing, but I know a guy who'd be happy to accompany you."

"A skating rink just opened on the Peveril Leisure Park. Can you skate?"

"Me?" I laughed. "You must be kidding."

"Me neither. It might be fun, and then a drink afterwards. How about the day after tomorrow?"

The bell rang.

"Sure. Why not."

The second thing I noticed about Charlie was the annoying way he played continuously with a small silver coin. The first thing was his dayglow top. He was no looker, but you wouldn't lose him in the dark.

"How about we hook up afterwards?" He certainly didn't lack confidence.

The coin dropped onto the table and I grabbed it.

"Give that back to me, please." Confident Charlie had suddenly disappeared. In his place was nervous, unsure of himself Charlie, who looked like he might burst into tears.

When I studied it more closely, I realised it wasn't a coin at all. I'd seen trinkets like that before on a market stall in Candlefield.

"Where did you get this?"

"What are you talking about?"

"Tell me where you got it or I'll be forced to break your fingers."

Do I know how to sweet talk a guy or what?

Nervous Charlie was too shocked to argue. He gave me all the information I needed, and then scurried away as soon as the bell rang.

"Hi, I'm Cedric."

"Goodbye, Cedric."

Mrs V was snoring like a trooper when I walked into the office—her head resting on the desk. She had obviously been knitting into the early hours of the morning. The woman was determined to bankrupt me. My only consolation was that Maxwell was going to have to match me pound for pound. We could declare bankruptcy together—how romantic.

"Morning, Mrs V," I shouted.

"What? Who? Where am I?" She replaced her glasses which had slid onto the desk. "Jill? I must have fallen asleep."

"Why didn't you go home?"

"I can sleep when I—"

"Don't say that."

"I was going to say, when I've finished the scarf-a-thon. What time is it, anyway?"

"A little after nine."

"Time's up then. I'd better take this—hold on—where is it?"

"Where's what?"

"The scarf, of course."

I shrugged.

"It was here before I fell asleep. Someone must have stolen it."

And I knew who.

I rushed into my office. The scarf was tied to one leg of my desk. From there it stretched to, and out of, the open window. Just as I suspected.

"What are you doing?" I called down to Winky who

was swinging on the other end of the scarf.

"What does it look like?"

"It looks like you're stuck."

"This stupid thing isn't long enough."

"Good thing too. It's already going to cost me a small fortune."

"Your financial travails are all very interesting," Winky said, "but in case it has escaped your notice, I'm in mortal danger. Call the rescue services. Quickly!"

That conversation would go well.

*'A cat you say? Hanging from a scarf, you say?'*

I legged it downstairs.

"Let go, and I'll catch you," I shouted up to Winky.

"How do I know you won't drop me?"

"You're going to have to trust me."

"Why don't you lie down on the floor, and I can fall onto your body?"

"I'm going to count to five then you jump. If you don't, I leave you there."

"Are you any good at catch?"

"Five."

"There's still time to call the rescue services."

"Four."

"If I die, I'll haunt you."

"Three."

Who knew a cat could weigh so much. It was just as well I'd cast the 'power' spell before he'd let go of the scarf.

I kept a tight grip on Winky, in case he tried to make a break for it. Overhead, I could see Mrs V pulling the scarf back through the window.

"She's going to kill you," I said, as I walked back up the stairs.

"Let her try. I'll use my kung fu moves on her."

"Since when did you know kung fu?"

"I've been taking a correspondence course."

Of course. I should have known.

"He didn't mean any harm," I said to Mrs V.

"Cats will be cats." She smiled.

Winky and I exchanged looks. *'Cats will be cats?'*

"Quick," he whispered. "Take me next door before she changes her mind."

I did as he asked, then went back to check on Mrs V. "Are you sure you're okay?"

"Of course. Why wouldn't I be?"

"Winky? The scarf?" I'd lost the ability to string together even a simple sentence.

"He did me a favour. The scarf is a foot longer now. More money for a good cause."

Yay!

'Harry Tinsel's Magic Shop' was on a small back street, just off the high street in Washbridge. The window was stacked high with all manner of cheap magic tricks: marked cards, magic rope, magic cup and ball. Mikey would have loved it.

A bell sounded on the door as I entered. The interior was even smaller than it appeared from outside.

"Good morning, madam." The man behind the counter had more hair on his chin than on the top of his head. I could sense he was a wizard.

"Good morning."

"Is there anything in particular you're looking for

today?"

"It's a little embarrassing." I looked around as though there might be someone lurking nearby.

"I see." He clearly didn't.

"I'm having difficulty—" Another look around—just for effect. "Getting a date."

I had hoped he might look a little more surprised that I couldn't get a date.

"I'm very sorry to hear that, but I'm not sure how I can help. Maybe a dating agency?"

"Good idea. Perhaps I should try speed dating. I believe some of your customers do."

His expression changed. He knew the game was up.

"I don't know what you mean," he stuttered.

"I think you do. Maybe I should call someone to jog your memory. A Rogue Retriever?"

"No! Please, don't do that! Please, I'm begging you!" Tears ran down his cheeks as he continued to plead with me.

"How many Stor-a-Spells have you sold?" I said.

"Three."

I glared at him.

"Five then, certainly no more than eight. Ten at the most."

"What spell did you use?"

"'Attract'. I only did it as a favour the first time. One of my regular clients told me that he'd never had a date in his life. I felt sorry for him."

The spell had made the holder *attractive* to all members of the opposite sex. That in turn had given him a self-confidence he'd never known before.

"To the tune of?"

He looked puzzled.

"How much did you charge your friend?"

"Fifty pounds."

"Very generous. And the others? How did they find you?"

"Word of mouth. Other men saw the results, and asked what had caused the change in him."

"And how much did you charge the others?"

"A hundred pounds each."

"A nice little earner then?"

"Business has been quiet."

"Have you heard of Daze?"

"Please don't call her. Please! I'm too old to go to prison."

Call me a big, old softy, but I genuinely felt sorry for the guy. Sure, he'd been making money, but he'd also given a few men the confidence they needed to get a date. Even so, enough was enough.

"I won't call Daze if you promise that you won't sell any more Stor-a-Spells."

"I promise."

"And, you reverse the spells on all the ones you've already sold."

"But they'll stop working."

"That's the idea."

"They'll want their money back."

"They probably will. Do we have a deal or shall I give Daze a call?" I waved her business card in front of his face.

"We have a deal."

When I got back to my flat, I spotted a familiar figure in

the distance.

'Ivy' the Casanova had disappeared—in his place was Mr Ivers.

"Evening, Mr Ivers."

He'd been staring at his feet, and hadn't noticed my approach. "Oh, hello."

"Everything okay?" I asked.

"Err—yes—I think so."

"Good."

"I think I may have been a little rude to you lately," he said, in barely more than a whisper. "I'm very sorry. I don't know what came over me."

"Think nothing of it." I turned and made to walk away.

"Before you go."

"Yes?"

"I'm thinking of resurrecting my newsletter. Would you be interested in signing up?"

It was the least I could do.

# Chapter 24

Kathy's text arrived as I was about to set off for the office. It read: 'Pete has lost his job'.

Kathy loved to moan, and she usually thought nothing of getting on the phone to bend my ear. The fact that she hadn't called, had me worried. It wasn't like her, so I went straight around there.

Peter answered the door. "Hey, Jill. Shouldn't you be at work?"

"Sorry to hear about the job."

"It's okay, I'll find another one."

"Where?" Kathy shouted. "There aren't any jobs!"

"She isn't taking it very well." Peter forced a smile. "Do you want to come in?"

"Where are the kids?"

"The next door neighbour has taken them to school—we take their kids sometimes."

"I didn't mean for you to come round." Kathy was still in her dressing gown—never a good sign.

"Do the kids know?" I asked.

"I've told them," Peter said. "But they've got other things on their minds. Like the giraphant that Kathy made for Lizzie."

"How bad are things?" I took a seat next to Kathy at the breakfast bar.

"About as bad as they get."

"What about savings?"

"What savings?" Kathy's laugh was hollow.

"I can help," I said.

"We can't take your money," Peter said. "I'll find a job."

"They've laid everyone off at your old place." Kathy

picked at a fingernail. "They'll all be chasing the same jobs."

"Then I'll do something else."

"What? What can you do?"

Peter stared at Kathy.

"I'm sorry." She began to cry. "I didn't mean that."

"It's okay." Peter put his arm around her.

I felt like I was intruding. "I'd better get to the office. I'll catch up with you later."

I wasn't sure if they heard me leave or not.

I read the note that Mrs V had left on her desk. Apparently, she was going to be on TV.

I hurried to the coffee shop, three doors down because they kept their TV on all day. It was tuned into a twenty-four hour news station, but no one was watching it.

"Could I get a latte, please?"

"Anything else?"

"Do you have any blueberry muffins?"

"We do."

Damn it.

"I'll have a small one."

"They only come in one size."

"I'll take a small one."

"Anything else?"

"Could you change the channel, please? No one seems to be watching this."

"Sure. What did you want to watch?"

"Channel 381 — Wool TV."

"Bull TV?"

"Wool. You know." I did a quick impression of someone knitting, which seemed to leave him even more confused, but he switched the channel anyway.

Mrs V had been invited to make an appearance on Wool TV's morning show. Apparently she'd knitted the longest scarf in the well publicised scarf-a-thon. After I'd handed over my sponsorship money, Kathy and Peter might not be the only ones filing for bankruptcy.

I asked for the volume to be turned up, so I could hear the presenter.

"Yesterday, the winner of the scarf-a-thon, sponsored by Ever A Wool Moment, was announced, and I'm delighted to say that Annabel Versailles is with us today in our Washbridge studio." He turned around to face the screen behind him, on which Mrs V was adjusting her ear piece.

"Annabel? May I call you Annabel?"

"Is this thing working?" Mrs V continued to fiddle with her ear piece.

Quality TV.

"Annabel. This is Joe Stratford. Can you hear me?"

"When do we start?" She pulled out the ear piece.

A young man walked on screen, put the ear piece back into Mrs V's ear, and made some adjustment to the small controller fastened to her dress.

"Annabel?"

"Hello."

"Can you hear me now?"

"Yes, I can hear you."

The young man disappeared off-screen.

"Annabel, this is Joe Stratford."

"Hello, Joe." Mrs V blushed and came over all unnecessary. Clearly, she was a massive Joe Stratford fan.

"Welcome to the show, and congratulations on your

achievement. Do you have the scarf with you?"

"I do." She leaned forward, and picked it up.

"How long is it?" Joe asked.

"Just under twenty feet, Joe."

Twenty feet? Maths wasn't my strong suit, but twenty times twelve, that was two hundred and forty inches. At two pounds an inch, that was four hundred and eighty pounds. You have got to be kidding me.

"That's incredible," Joe gushed. "Tell me, Annabel, is there anywhere that people can see this magnificent scarf?"

"Yes, Joe. When I leave the studio, I'll be taking it to 'Ever A Wool Moment', which is located on the high street in Washbridge. It'll be on display there until the end of the month."

My grandmother, the marketing genius.

I left a note for Mrs V congratulating her on the scarf. I also mentioned that I was going to pay Colonel Briggs a visit.

"Hello again, young lady." Colonel Briggs met me at the door. "Do come in. Tea? Coffee? Something a little stronger, maybe?"

"Nothing for me thanks. I can't stay long."

"Story of my life. Pretty girls never could wait to get away from me."

"I don't believe that for a moment."

His grin gave him away. Colonel Briggs had almost certainly been a lady's man in his day.

"What can I do for you, Jill?"

"I wanted to let you know about the Vicars case. No

charges are going to be brought against Doctor Mills."

"Jolly pleased to hear it."

"You are? I thought you might have been disappointed."

"Not at all. As far as I can see, the doctor's only crimes were stupidity, and a love of his dog. I'm guilty of both of those. Living with the consequences of what he did will be punishment enough."

"What about the trophy? Will you take it off him?"

"Certainly not. It was the dog who won the trophy, and he's done nothing wrong. I do appreciate your driving all the way out here to tell me though."

"I did have an ulterior motive," I said.

"Maybe my old charm is still working after all." He grinned.

"There's no question about that, but that's not the reason I came either."

"How can I help you then?"

"Have you hired a new gardener yet?"

"Can't you tell? The borders are in a shocking state. I really need to get my finger out and find someone."

"I may be able to help."

"Oh?"

"My brother-in-law, Peter, is a landscape gardener. At least he was. He's been made redundant. I was wondering.—"

"Send him to see me tomorrow. If he's half as good a gardener as you are a private investigator, he'll have himself a job."

"Thank you, Colonel."

"My absolute pleasure."

I gave Kathy a call. "Kathy?"

"Oh, hi." She sounded just as depressed as when I'd seen her that morning.

"I might have found Peter a job."

"Really? What kind of job?"

I told her all about the Colonel, about his house, and most importantly about his gardens.

"He wants to see Peter tomorrow."

"He'll be there. Thanks, Jill. You're a diamond."

"No problem."

"Hey, by the way." Kathy already sounded as though a weight had been lifted off her shoulders. "Did you see Mrs V on the TV this morning?"

"I did."

"That scarf of hers was incredible. How long was it?"

"Too long."

I met Maxwell in the car park of the new ice rink which had been open for less than a month—the old one had closed over ten years ago.

"Are you sure you can't skate?" I asked.

"This is my first time."

"I'm not sure I believe you after the way you set me up at bowling."

"I set you up? You were the one who finished on three strikes."

"That's right." I grinned. "I did, didn't I? Maybe, I should buy my own bowling shirt. What should I have on it? 'Three Strikes Baby'?"

"Are you ever going to let me forget that?"

"Highly unlikely."

The ice rink was doing good business; the opening

offers had ensured the place was full.

"It's cold in here," Maxwell said as we stood rink-side.

"It's ice. What did you expect?"

"There are more people on the ice than I thought there would be," he said. "Maybe we should just watch."

"Chicken. Cluck, cluck."

"I was only thinking of you."

"That's so very considerate of you. Cluck, cluck—"

"Okay. Let's get some shoes."

"Shoes?" I laughed.

"Whatever they're called. Those things with the metal underneath."

We made our way over to the central desk where a pretty young woman, wearing a tee-shirt with the words 'Have an Ice Day' printed across her chest, jumped to attention. "How may I be of assistance today?"

I wondered how long such unbridled enthusiasm would last. A month? Six?

"My friend and I would like two pairs of those things with the metal underneath," I said.

Maxwell scowled at me.

"Size?"

"Six," I said.

"Same." Maxwell started to undo his boots.

"Six?"

"Yes. So?"

"You have women's feet."

"Tell me again why you had to resort to speed dating."

"I told you. I went there to work on a case."

"So says you."

We hobbled over to the rink.

"After you." I stepped aside.

Maxwell held onto the rail for grim death, as his feet tried desperately to go in opposite directions. "This is harder than it looks."

"I think you're supposed to let go of the rail," I said.

"Whose bright idea was this?" As he spoke, one of his legs slipped from under him, and he landed with a thud on his backside.

I laughed. "Sorry."

"You look it." He clambered back to his feet.

"Why don't we give it a go?" I said. "I'll go first."

"Okay, but don't go too fast."

I let go of the side, and took slow, deliberate steps, with my arms held out wide for balance. "Come on!" I called back to him.

He released his grip on the side, and tried to get his balance. After a few moments, he took one hesitant step, and then another.

"Come on." I held out a hand, but he didn't see it because his gaze was fixed on his feet.

Thud! He hit the ice again. That had to hurt.

"Are you okay?" I asked, the smile on my face threatening to turn into laughter.

"This is stupid." He slipped again when he attempted to stand.

"Why don't we hold hands?" I said. "We can help each other to balance."

"Okay." He took my hand, and we made our way slowly around the edge of the rink. Kids, no more than five years of age, came flying past us.

"How do they do that?" Maxwell grumbled.

"What?"

"Skate so fast. And jump and twirl like that?"

"You mean like this?" I let go of his hand and glided away, building speed as I went. My toe-loop was a little rusty, but I landed the axel perfectly. After one lap of the rink, I slid to a halt in front of Maxwell.

"I suppose you think that's funny!" he said, stern faced.

"Actually, yeah."

"Why didn't you tell me you could skate?"

"Why didn't you tell me you could bowl?"

He cracked a smile. "I guess I deserved that. Quits?"

"Quits."

"It's not funny," Maxwell was shuffling around on the seat. We'd abandoned the skating, and were in the adjoining bar.

"It kind of is."

He'd taken so many falls on the ice that he could hardly bear to sit.

"When did you learn to skate?"

"When I was a kid. Kathy used to go dancing, but I couldn't see the appeal. Dad took me skating instead. I won a few medals."

"Why did you give it up?"

"The old rink closed down. The nearest one was sixty miles away. And besides, I'd more or less grown out of it by then."

"I probably won't be able to walk in the morning." He shifted position again.

"Never mind. I have some news which is guaranteed to cheer you up."

"Go on."

"Mrs V's scarf came in at just under twenty feet."

# Chapter 25

Mrs V came through to my office.

"Everything okay?" I asked.

"Mr Roberts is here. He looks different."

"Different how? Don't tell me he's wearing a coloured tie."

"Shall I send him in?"

"Yes, please." Now, I was intrigued.

What the? Either I'd slipped into some psychedelic, parallel universe or Mr Robert Roberts, my accountant, had been smoking the funny tobacco.

"Hi!" he said.

Hi? Robert Roberts was many things, but he was not the kind of man who said 'Hi'.

Something very strange had occurred. Mr Robert Roberts had undergone a scary transformation. Mr Robert Roberts had turned into a hipster.

"Mr Roberts?" I managed, once the initial shock had passed. "I almost didn't recognise you."

"Do you like the threads?"

"Very nice. I didn't think you were due to call yet."

"That's true. True that is."

He had to have been smoking something.

"I've given up the accountancy practice."

"Oh? What about my books?"

"I've left all your accounts and papers with the good lady out there. I'm sure you'll find someone to take them over. It's not as though you have much income to account for."

Thanks for the reminder. "What are you going to do instead?"

"I'm now a food critic."

"Really. That's quite a career change."

"I suppose so." He scratched his hipster beard.

"Well, thanks for popping in to tell me. Maybe I'll see you around."

He looked me slowly up and down. "Unlikely."

Cheek!

"You have to see it, Jill." Mrs V had been on my case for most of the day.

It wasn't that I minded going to Ever A Wool Moment; I was just worried that I might bump into Grandma. My next lesson was in a couple of days, and I was behind on my studies. Mrs V's scarf-a-thon scarf was on display in the shop. The scarf that had cost me the best part of five hundred pounds.

"If it isn't my star pupil." Grandma collared me as soon as I set foot in the door of her wool emporium. "What brings you here? The wine offer has finished."

"I didn't come for the—I came to see Mrs V's scarf-a-thon scarf."

"You mean Costa?"

"What?"

"That's what I've decided to call the scarf."

"Oh? Okay."

"Wouldn't you like to know why?"

"Not really."

"I'll tell you anyway. I called it Costa because it costa you five hundred pounds in sponsorship. Get it?"

"Hilarious."

"I thought so."

"So where is Costa?"

"Follow me." She led me to the back of the shop. There, just above the pay desk was a huge glass cabinet. Inside it was Costa—looking like a huge red python. Next to the cabinet, an illuminated display flashed the words 'Scarf-a-thon - Costa, by Annabel Versailles.'

After a few moments, Grandma had lost interest in me, and was chatting to some of the customers who were waiting to pay. The queue stretched all the way back to the door.

"Hi," I said to one of the assistants. "You're busy today."

"It's been like this all week—ever since the 'everlasting' arrived."

"Everlasting?"

"It's a new concept apparently. I don't know how it works, but these balls of wool never run out."

"That's impossible."

"That's what I said, but apparently it's true."

"How can Grandma make money if the wool lasts forever?"

"It's sold on subscription. Like Spotify and Netflix."

I knew nothing about knitting, but I knew BS when I smelled it. "Can I see one?"

"Sure." She skipped across the shop, and seconds later came back with a ball of red everlasting wool.

"How much is this?" I asked.

"One colour is one pound per month. Two colours are—"

"One colour should be enough."

I filled in the paperwork for my subscription, and left with my ball of everlasting wool. If this turned out to be what I thought it was, I might have a way to get Grandma out of my life, or at least out of Washbridge.

"Did you see the scarf?" Mrs V asked, as soon as I walked back into the office.
"Costa?"
"Who?"
"Never mind. Yes, it's looking good. You should be proud."
She beamed.
"Mrs V. Would you do me a favour? Can you knit me something using this wool?" I handed her the everlasting wool.
"Is this from your grandmother's shop?"
"It is. It's a new line."
"What would you like me to make for you?"
"How about a scarf?"
"Is this all the wool you have? I won't get far on only one ball."
"Give it a try. Let me know how you get on."

I know, I know. Grandma is my flesh and blood, blah, blah, blah. But, she is also one colossal pain in the rear. What if someone, not me obviously, but someone were to let Daze know that a certain someone was using magic to sell so-called everlasting wool? Wouldn't that certain someone be made to return to Candlefield for flaunting their magic in public? Purely hypothetically of course. Cue evil laugh.

I'd spoken to Daze about The Dark One after Amber had been abducted. She'd suggested we meet to discuss what we could do. We'd agreed to keep the meeting low key; that's why we'd arranged to meet at Cuppy C. It was the first time I'd seen Daze wearing her catsuit since the very first time we met in the same place. She looked great.

Daze had commandeered the table in the far corner of the tea room, away from prying eyes and ears. Amber and Pearl were both behind the counter. Daze had asked them to give us some time alone. No one argued with Daze. Except me, apparently.

"Doing what you've been doing up to now clearly isn't working," I said.

Daze's face flushed red. "Who do you think you're talking to? I'm not some jobsworth cop who doesn't give a damn."

"I'm sorry. I'm just frustrated that no one seems to know anything, and no one seems to be doing anything about it."

"The police are a waste of time, so you can forget them. The sup sups have the powers to overcome TDO, but we have to find him or her first."

"Her?"

"That's the whole point. After all of these years, we still don't know who he or she is. How are we meant to combat an enemy when we don't have a clue who they are? That's where you come in. We need someone who can identify TDO. We can take it from there."

"But if no one has managed to identify him so far, what makes you think I can?"

"Apparently, TDO wants you dead. There has to be a reason for that. Maybe he is scared of you."

"Yeah, right."

"Find the reason why he wants you dead, and maybe you'll find out who he or she is. What do you say?"

"What do I have to lose?" I shrugged. "He wants me dead anyway, so at least this way I get to fight back."

"You can't tell anyone what you're doing."

"That's okay. Maxine Jewell has already made it clear she doesn't want me working on her patch—I'm used to working around the police."

"Not just the police. You can't tell anyone. Not your grandma, aunt or the twins. No one. This is between you and me. Agreed?"

"Agreed."

Daze was about to call the twins over when I took her arm. "Hold on a second. I may have a case for you—a witch using magic for personal gain in the human world."

"Give me the details."

"Just give me a moment; I need to make a quick phone call."

I walked over to the window, and called Mrs V.

"It's Jill. I wanted to check how you were getting on with the wool I left with you."

"Okay, dear, but you'll have to get more if you want me to finish this scarf. I've run out."

"Are you sure?"

"I think I'd know."

"Yeah. Of course. Okay, I'll see you soon."

Daze had her notebook in her hand. "Well?"

"Cancel that. Looks like I got it wrong." Somehow Grandma had got one over on me again. She must have known what I was up to. One day, I'd get my own back—you just see if I don't.

If there's one thing I hated more than weddings, it was looking at photos of weddings. Amber and Pearl must have taken two zillion photos of Mum's wedding. Not satisfied with those, they'd also got all of the ones that their fiancés had taken too. After Daze and I had finished the official TDO business, the twins had come over to join us. Since then, I'd been subjected to an hour of mind-blowing dullness.

"Pink suits you," Daze teased.

"It wasn't my choice," I said. "I was ambushed."

The twins took it in turns to show a photo. I was on my second coffee—it was only the caffeine that was keeping me awake.

"Who's that?" Daze pointed to the photo on Amber's phone.

"That's Jill's boyfriend."

"His name is Drake, and he's very hot," Pearl said.

"He isn't my boyfriend. We've been out a couple of times, that's all."

The twins grinned inanely at me.

"What? We're just friends."

Daze took my arm, and said, "Can I have a word?"

Anything to get away from the twins.

When we were out of earshot, she said in little more than a whisper, "I know Drake. I arrested him three years ago."

Oh bum!

# ALSO BY ADELE ABBOTT

## The Witch P.I. Mysteries:

*Witch Is When... (Books #1 to #12)*
Witch Is When It All Began
Witch Is When Life Got Complicated
Witch Is When Everything Went Crazy
Witch Is When Things Fell Apart
Witch Is When The Bubble Burst
Witch Is When The Penny Dropped
Witch Is When The Floodgates Opened
Witch Is When The Hammer Fell
Witch Is When My Heart Broke
Witch Is When I Said Goodbye
Witch Is When Stuff Got Serious
Witch Is When All Was Revealed

*Witch Is Why... (Books #13 to #24)*
Witch Is Why Time Stood Still
Witch is Why The Laughter Stopped
Witch is Why Another Door Opened
Witch is Why Two Became One
Witch is Why The Moon Disappeared
Witch is Why The Wolf Howled
Witch is Why The Music Stopped
Witch is Why A Pin Dropped
Witch is Why The Owl Returned
Witch is Why The Search Began
Witch is Why Promises Were Broken
Witch is Why It Was Over

**The Susan Hall Mysteries:**
Whoops! Our New Flatmate Is A Human.
Whoops! All The Money Went Missing.
Whoops! There's A Canary In My Coffee
*See web site for availability.*


**AUTHOR'S WEB SITE**
http:www.AdeleAbbott.com

**FACEBOOK**
http://www.facebook.com/AdeleAbbottAuthor

**MAILING LIST**
(new release notifications only)
http:/AdeleAbbott.com/adele/new-releases/

Printed in Great Britain
by Amazon